Nathaniel's Firepit

Rebecca A. Espinoza

For Victor

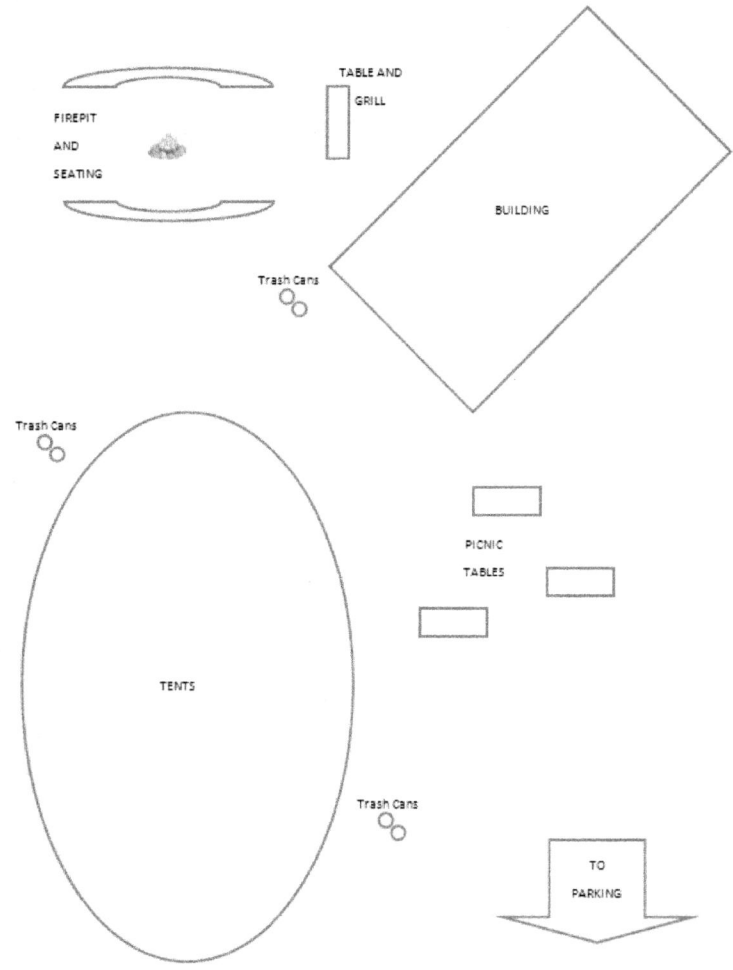

Contents

Prologue

"You're going to do what?" Cassandra stared at her son.

"I am starting a campsite business in the area with Ethan," replied Nathaniel.

"But you are both completely ignorant of the outdoors. You know nothing at all about making it outside a city! You do not even own a pair of hiking boots!"

"YouTube! Library! Google! Experience! We can figure it out. And we've saved the money to get started. We'll use the old campsite that Ethan inherited from his great-great-aunt, so we can start by focusing on that place. We have already started straightening it up. A road to the campsite is already there. A good building with running water and electricity is there. It has cell phone service. It is not exactly 'the outdoors.' Ethan and I can help guests set up tents and then do campfire stories and s'mores. Or something. It'll be a weekend thing to start, so you don't even have to worry about helping me pay the rent."

"No, no, no, no, no, no. Not the business. You know I will support you in whatever you want.... "

"As long as it is legal and ethical," they intoned at the same time.

Cassandra continued, "There is a reason that Belinay abandoned that campsite to her sister. Ethan would never have inherited otherwise. Things have happened there."

"Are you starting up with the ley lines and the portals and the enchanted rituals and the mythical creatures again? Really? We're in the 21st century. Isn't it time you stopped with that?"

"Belinay's campsite is likely in pretty good condition considering it has not been used for decades. Have you not considered why nothing deteriorates there? And I was there! These things happened to me and to Belinay."

Nathaniel's eye roll must have given him an inside view of his skull. "Ethan and I are doing this. It will be all right. And if any of your silly imaginings from the shenanigans of your good old days start happening, we will reconsider. By the way, we are calling the business Nathaniel's Firepit."

Cassandra stared at her son, the apprehension shining in her eyes.

"I have to get back to work. Thank you for lunch." Nathaniel gave his mom a hug and a quick kiss on the top of her head.

After watching him drive away, Cassandra turned to the corner of her kitchen, where the ghost of Belinay showed itself sitting on the charmed wooden stool.

"You knew the cycle would start up again," Belinay said.

"Of course, I did. I just don't want my son to go through what we did."

"It's in his blood. You never told him what you really are. And how incredibly strong you are. And as my sister's descendant, it is in Ethan's blood as well. I am not sure if Ethan has ever tried to learn how to use any abilities. Nathaniel showed potential when he was a child, though."

"I did try to tell him, but Nathaniel is a skeptic. Just like his father. And his father died in the last cycle. I cannot bear to lose my son as well. Not that anyone believes anymore that the fae interbreed with humans. As Nathaniel said, it's the 21st century. Magic is scientific explanations. But it was not all magic. Some of it was just not earthly."

"Yet, you ARE interspecies, as was his father, although he was not fae. It was that darkness from his non-human side that got Nathaniel's father killed, not the beings themselves. And Nathaniel's father was skeptical because HIS father never understood what his mother was, or that bearing a human child would be fatal to her. I don't think Nathaniel is as skeptical as you imagine. He has always accepted me as a ghost, even when he couldn't talk about it outside of this house. Ethan started believing when I showed myself to him after my death."

"Did you pop this idea into Ethan's head?"

"I had to. I can feel the cycle starting again, and the only two that I know that could help in this are Ethan and Nathaniel. Others will be drawn to the campsite, so they are not alone. They will also have us. Neither of us had any real backup when it was our turn."

Cassandra groaned. "How much time do we have?"

"I wish I knew." And with that, Belinay disappeared.

The Thought Vampire

Nathaniel's Firepit, Sixteen Months Later

"….the steps came closer. And closer. And CLOSER," Nathaniel looked around and noticed the fear in several of the children's eyes, as well as a couple of adults. He was going to have to change the ending. "When the steps came up right behind Little Gray-Eyes, the child turned slowly around, and saw…."

Everyone leaned closer, prepared to be frightened.

"His best friend carrying the hot chocolate."

The laughter was unusually nervous this time. Nathaniel and Ethan exchanged a worried look. This was not the expected reaction. Usually the laughter was good-natured, with a few groans and eye rolls thrown in. Nathaniel had noticed that uneasiness among campers had been growing over the last couple of weeks. The adults had been retreating to the tents with their children as soon as story-time was over instead of lingering around the firepit to chat. When he had seen older children that he thought could handle the scarier endings, the screams had been more *insistent*. And neither he nor Ethan had been exactly themselves. They struggled to set up, even with the checklists, often forgetting small details. They lost track of time. They often felt exhausted. They, um, they ….

A woman had tramped up to Ethan stamping her hiking boots like a toddler. Her glare was strong enough to make Ethan back up a step, but he still raised his unibrow in question to help her.

"Excuse me, but I see everyone is heading off to sleep. Wasn't there supposed to be a children's story-time? I paid for that," She looked pretty teed off.

"Yes, we just finished it," Ethan was confused.

"Oh. I must have dozed off. Not a very good story if it cannot keep someone awake," she said and stomped off with a scowl to her tent.

"What was that all about?" Nathaniel approached Ethan.

"Oh, she was upset because, um, she thought…. You know, I can't remember," replied Ethan. He shrugged and headed back to the small building that he and Nathaniel had put up on the campsite. The building served as office, first aid center, and supply house. It had cots for Nathaniel and Ethan to sleep, as well as a bathroom with a shower for them. Nathaniel felt disquieted, but followed Ethan to the building without thinking about it anymore.

At the edge of the campsite, Belinay's ghost closed her eyes, shook her head and sighed. At least, as much as a ghost CAN sigh. She had come up to the campsite since it had opened to enjoy the stories. Ok, she was standing guard because she expected the worst. "I hope it is not a thought vampire." Then she hurried herself off to talk to Cassandra. No one noticed her. No one noticed the shadow-like being that attached itself to her. No one noticed when that shadow-like being detached itself and advanced towards the 19-year-old, Cameron, whose last name also happened to be Cameron. Ms. Cameron felt a slight dizziness.

****

That was not a word that usually came out of Cassandra's mouth. Suddenly seeing Belinay's ghost sitting on the toilet after stepping out of the shower had caused a bit of sudden concern.

"I have to leave for work in thirty minutes," Cassandra stated.

"No problem. I will explain while you get ready," Belinay grinned. "I will ride along with you to finish discussing." The look Cassandra gave her verified that she did NOT want to deal with something so complicated that it required a passenger. It meant that the cycle had restarted.

Cassandra was grateful that technology had advanced so that when people stared at her talking to what appeared as an empty vehicle, they assumed that she was on a call. Way back in the day, she either looked nuts or had to pretend she was singing. "So, tell me again what is a thought vampire?"

Belinay was getting irritated, "I haven't encountered one in decades. Vampires are any creature that sucks life force from you. The most common are the blood suckers. They are easy to deal with. But your blood is not the only life force. Your memories are central to who you are as a person. Thought vampires make you forget things. They start fairly weak, such as making you miss a step in a process, or not really paying attention when you are driving, or feeling disoriented in a store. But each memory they take makes them stronger. People they attack then think they slept through something, or cannot recall specific actions. In the worst cases, the person will lose consciousness. Fortunately, they can only attack one person at a time and are unable to reproduce."

Cassandra shivered, "Does a person ever recover?"

Belinay nodded, "Almost always. The human brain is amazing, so most of the memories either return or the person is fully aware of them missing. Can't tell you how they impact animals. I don't know if they can impact non-Earthlings."

"How do they travel?"

"I don't know"

"How do you stop them?

"I don't know."

"What do they look like?"

"I don't know."

"How do you know when a person has been attacked instead of a medical issue?"

"I don't know."

"Are there people who are more likely to be attacked?"

"I suspect it would be those with anger issues, just like with every other type of creature."

"What are we going to do?"

"I don't know."

"How bad can this thing get?"

"I don't know."

"Is my son in danger?"

"Probably."

Casandra focused on driving. She had a busy day at work, but felt she would notice any little detail that was—not quite right. She would notice not just with herself, but with her co-workers. She hoped she did not become terribly paranoid because of this. But just kinda paranoid was OK?!

More importantly: How was she going to convince Nathaniel that this was happening?

****

Token Village wasn't actually big enough to be considered a village, nor had it ever been incorporated. It did not have signs directing a person to it, nor would you find it on any map. Several houses existed in the vicinity, but the owners did not consider themselves part of Token Village. Token Village consisted of a general store, a gas station, and a jail. An odd thing about Token Village was that these three buildings never seemed to need repairs, or new supplies for that matter.

The jail had a main area with two desks, four chairs, two filing cabinets, and a small table as a coffee station. This room was covered in hideous brown carpet. Rumor had it that if the carpet was ever deep cleaned, it would turn out to be green. Only one jail cell existed in the place, and that remained empty year-round, as no one was sure where the key had gone.

Detective Jerome Nickel sat behind one the desks. He had been the only police officer in Token Village for twenty-three years, the whole time with the job title of Detective. It had been the only place that had given him an interview when he graduated from the police academy. The previous Detective was retiring after fifty years and had offered Detective Nickel the job on the spot. In the entire time, he had never needed to investigate anything more than missing pets. He wasn't sure he would know what to do if he did.

At the other desk sat Cheshire, who had been there since, well, a very long time. Cheshire was the office manager, a job that consisted of sitting at the desk. On occasion, a piece of paper would need to go into a file cabinet, or older documents taken out and put into a box, and sent to the county. Cheshire insisted that any references to said person be as "Cheshire," never giving an actual name. The nickname had been picked up from an apparent inability to stop smiling. Obviously.

Neither of them was aware of where the bi-weekly paychecks came from or how the office bills were paid, and didn't care. They both lived in nearby cities. They did not often talk to each other, as there was nothing much to talk about. In twenty-three years, they knew everything they could possibly want to know about each other. They each drank pots and pots of coffee and stayed on-line to pass the time. They had both been known to read entire novels in a day. They had played board games, but that stopped when Detective Nickel realized that he always lost. Neither could remember the last time the phone had rang, except for a reminder of expired car warranties.

Detective Nickel was currently seated in front of Cameron (no middle name) Cameron. This one had been causing trouble for him since the missing kitten case six years ago. Then there was the missing chicken case five years ago. And the missing …. "Ms. Cameron, I picked you up standing with the spray paint in your hand, in front of the jail wall you defaced. I can get camera footage from the general store. And you are telling me you can't remember?" She had never done anything this serious before, that he knew of. Vandalism was serious in Token Village. Then he noticed something he had never noticed in her before. Anxiety.

Cameron spoke up, "I can't remember. I honestly only remember that I was bored out of my gourd and got in the car to go to the General Store. I remember buying the spray paint, and then I was being led over here to the jailhouse. Everything in between is a complete blank. And the General Store does not have cameras." Her usual defiance was gone, replaced with teary eyes. She truly was worried about a memory lapse. At nineteen, she should be, if it had really happened.

Nickel just didn't want to deal with it. "Let's look at the damage and see how you can clean it up." But when they went outside, the wall had no paint nor any sign that it had been painted. Nickel knew this had been likely, because Token Village buildings were undamageable. He turned to see Cameron running up the hill.

When Nickel returned to his desk, Cheshire looked over and commented, "A bit of an escalation for her, isn't it?" Nickel gave Cheshire a blank look. He seemed not to know what Cheshire was talking about. Cheshire continued, "Ms. Cameron and the spray paint?" Nickel just shook his head, not understanding, and turned back to the computer.

Cheshire had seen the shadow-like thing move from Ms. Cameron to Detective Nickel. Quietly picking up a sticky note, Cheshire wrote out a reminder to try to reach Belinay's ghost. Failing that, pay a visit to Cassandra. Cheshire was not sure if a thought vampire could impact a non-human being as long-lived as Cheshire was, but no risk should be taken. As has often been stated: Put it in writing.

****

Eleven-year-old Johnny had not regained consciousness since arriving at the emergency room. With his youth, his mind worked efficiently, and the thought vampire had gorged on the electrical impulses that converted to thoughts. Lucky for him, the disruption was temporary. No one knew this yet, but he would gain back complete function within a day. He would never have any memory of what happened. His parents, however, would have nightmares for years.

They had been driving for several minutes after picking up snackage at the General Store they often took a detour for. It was an odd thing that whatever they craved at the moment could be found there. Then, Johnny had asked when they would get to the store. Immediately after, he asked when they would be leaving to go home. Then, he stopped talking and simply stared. His eyes slowly became opaque as he lost his thoughts. By the time they had reached the emergency room, Johnny was unresponsive. The parents would never know what a thought vampire was.

****

The thought vampire had traveled to the General Store while attached to Detective Nickel when he had gone to buy lunch. Nickel had not provided the thought vampire much sustenance. His mind was dulled by the monotony and boredom of his work days. The thought vampire had felt Johnny's mind, which was always whirling with curiosity. It had not hesitated to jump over. The thought vampire was not capable of thinking for itself. It could only sense and react. Johnny had been a sensible reaction.

The amount of electronic equipment was overwhelming in this building. The thought vampire would have called it drunkenness if it had any concept of that state. It thrived on the electrical impulses in human brains, but could feel all the artificial electrical impulses and was gaining too much power too fast. It jumped from Johnny to a nurse, who stood staring at a chart for close to fifteen minutes. Then from the nurse to a visitor, who could not figure out how to get out of the building. From the visitor to a patient leaving in a car, who believed that the "nap" was not the least bit restful. From the patient to the person driving the patient home. From the driver to the homeless person sleeping at the side of the convenience store where the driver went in to ask for directions. Here, with an unfortunate soul whose brain was working at a lower level, it let itself rest. The homeless person would never wake up.

The thought vampire needed to return to the fire. It had come through the fire drawn to the enhanced thoughts that occur when humans feel fear. It could not survive long in this plane as it did not have mass and was made up of energy. Too much energy would cause it to dissipate dramatically. Not enough energy would leave it drained, eternally, unable to move. It could only return to its world from the same place it exited. It felt where that was, but was unable to process thoughts, ironically, in order to navigate.

****

Cassandra had not been sure where the tapping had come from at first. She decided to ignore it, in the hopes she did not have another squirrel in the attic. Cheshire had arrived about ten minutes earlier. Then, the person outside had pounded five times on the door, making her jump. She opened the door in anger, "**WHAT!!**"

Cameron backed up a few steps when she saw literal lightning flashes in Cassandra's eyes. Sheesh. She had forgotten the rumors of Cassandra's ancestry. But she wasn't of solid Scottish blood herself for no reason. Cameron lifted her chin and said, "I think your son's campsite is causing problems. You need to fix it."

Cassandra immediately became suspicious of how Cameron would know about the campsite. She knew Cameron was always exploring, but did not have time to ask. Behind Cameron, Nathaniel and Ethan drove up in Edgar, a black car way too obnoxious to not be named. They ran up the front steps, past Cameron, into the living room and turned to face Cassandra. "Mom, there is some weird stuff going on at the firepit. Ethan wondered if you could talk to Belinay?"

"It happened at the jail as well." Cassandra had been listening to Cheshire's recitation of that morning's events when Cameron had arrived.

"What happened at the jail?" Nathaniel wasn't in the mood for this.

"I supposedly spray-painted the outside wall, but couldn't remember any of it. When Detective Nickel and I went outside, the wall was fine. At that point the memories flooded back, so I ran here," Cameron felt no guilt for the non-damage. It was not the first time those walls had repaired themselves from her handiwork.

"After that, Detective Nickel couldn't remember that you had been there. Which is too bad, because his report would have given me a couple of seconds worth of work in filing." The pout could be heard in Cheshire's voice. "I agree that we need Belinay."

"You can all stop talking about me as if I weren't here," Belinay said from the door where she had made herself visible. Cameron gasped and jumped behind Ethan. A huge guy like that should provide some protection. She could deal with lightning eyes, but ghosts? Ghosts were an entirely different story.

Nathaniel smirked at Cameron, at the same time he realized that Ethan didn't seem fazed. Nathaniel had grown up with his mom after all, and he remembered Belinay from his childhood. Ethan must know her as well, though they had never discussed it. Ethan was a descendent of Belinay, after all. "Ms. Belinay, ma'am. Good to mostly see through you," Nathaniel joked.

"Don't think I cannot still smack the smart-aleck out of you, you little whippersnapper." But Belinay was smiling at him. Nathaniel smiled back. Cheshire kept smiling. Cassandra and Ethan grinned at the reunion. Cameron thought the situation was ridiculous.

"Can someone PLEASE tell me what is going on?" Cameron was not having this anymore.

Everyone looked at her, and then as one, turned and stared at Belinay.

****

The conversation had centered around the history of the campsite first. Where the firepit was located was a portal. Though the Earth side never changed, the other opening would vary in different worlds. Not all of them were habitable to humans, though humans had traveled to many of the ones that were habitable. Every once in a while, inhabitants of the other worlds came to ours. Not all of the travelers were happy campers. The fire at the campsite could be a call to these other world inhabitants, and it was always a way to send them out. One hoped they went back to the same world they had come from.

Belinay's grandparents had come through the firepit portal from a world at war, and decided to stay Earth-side. They had used what Earthlings called "magic" to secure the area. Over the decades, other extra-terrestrial beings and half-terrestrial beings had been attracted to the area and settled. Many moved to other places around the world. Humans with stronger mental abilities had also traveled from other places on Earth to benefit from the firepit's power. Now, the campsite and surrounding area were a place that regular humans could visit, remember, but never want to linger.

As for the thought vampire, Belinay had no idea about it other than oral history of what it was. She might have come across one in her childhood, but she really couldn't remember. There might be a way to send one back, but she really couldn't remember. It was possible one could be very dangerous if attacked, but she really couldn't remember. She was certain that one could be tracked, but how, she really couldn't remember. Cheshire could see it, but wasn't sure if tracking it was possible. Belinay also couldn't really remember how to lure one back to the firepit. She suspected that it had been able to cling to her because manifesting used the same type of energy as thinking. But since she no longer had thoughts the same way a living person did, it had not impacted her.

Those around the table did not feel enlightened. "This is good pizza," Ethan said as he continued eating. They had ordered food, but except for Ethan, not found themselves hungry.

Nathaniel stared at Ethan and asked, "Does it follow random thinkers or do you think it is more likely to go after straight-forward thinking? For control purposes, I mean." Ethan stopped chewing when he became aware that everyone was looking at him in speculation. Then he shrugged and continued demolishing the food.

"One way to find out," said Cassandra.

****

Cheshire had bought the van fifteen years ago and then painted it a shade called Autumn Dreamscape. Cheshire said the color was a reminder of home. Most agreed it looked more like Cinderella's coach had used rotting pumpkins. It was the vehicle that fit all five physical beings and one formerly physical entity. So off they headed to the nearest town.

Cameron was driving, slowly, after she neglected to let the others know that she had never done so before. She knew that the gas was on the right and the brakes on the left. Good thing the van was an automatic. Cheshire was looking out the windows in hopes of spying the creature. Cassandra and Nathaniel looked for people that might show the kind of behavior that would indicate an attack. This was not easy because neither of them knew what that would look like. And people could just be weird to start with. Belinay was flickering, unusually tired from making herself visible. Ethan was scrunched up on the last seat of the van, somewhat worried about what they had volunteered him for.

"There!" Shouted Cheshire. From a convenience store, flashing red and blue lights appeared in the dark. In the middle of them, Cheshire explained, there was a darker shadow. Cameron went down the street a bit and pulled over to the curb. Nathaniel looked at Ethan, the question in his eyes. Ethan took a deep breath and nodded. The group knew they would be unable to approach the store. So Belinay decided to act as invisible bait.

****

No one was able to see Belinay as she searched for the thought vampire. Unlike Cheshire, she couldn't see it or sense it. What if it had gone into a police officer?

It seemed like she was the one that had carried it to Cameron in her wanderings through town. If she wasn't? If it was one of the campers? She had no memory loss from the campsite to the jail wall. She did remember it had been more difficult to wander. Then again, her energy was not the same as when she had lived. Suddenly, she felt heavier. Belinay thought that must be it. If Cheshire was not back in the van, she might have had some help seeing it.

The thought vampire felt an energy that seemed *familiar*. It grabbed the energy, but it could not feed from it. The energy was moving away from the other energies that could feed it, if it could get to them. Then a softer energy came in contact with it. It began to feed slowly.

Belinay had floated to Ethan and hugged him. Then her energy had just died out. And she was gone.

Cheshire saw Belinay go to Ethan. The dark shadow clinging to her jumped to Ethan, and she disappeared. Cheshire could always see Belinay, even when she was not manifesting. She couldn't, NO, she couldn't be gone. Cheshire tamped down the bad feelings, nodded to the others. Ethan was helped to the loading area in the back of the van. He was grinning and staring off into space.

****

Nathaniel was glad this was not a customer night. Imagine a thought vampire running loose in a group of guests. Again? Nathaniel remembered the woman that had questioned Ethan. It had been there last weekend, according to Belinay. Imagine believing in a thought vampire and extra-terrestrials. Forget UFOS. Portals were a better transport method. His stomach turned when he realized exactly how many extra-terrestrials had come through here. How many had come through other portals? How many were still around? Why had he never considered this before?

And the problem this particular one was causing in making the others lug big Ethan around. Goodness, the man was heavy. Nathaniel wondered just how much Ethan worked out at the gym. And if he would have weighed less if he had not eaten one-and-a-half pizzas by himself. The four were more than happy to just drop the man in front of the firepit. *THUNK.*

It seemed harder than usual to start the firepit. A coldness underneath it made it difficult. After several times, Nathaniel and Cameron did get it going. Ethan had starting slowly nodding his head.

"Now what?" Nathaniel asked. Everyone looked at each other.

"That was what Belinay was going to help with," Cassandra muttered.

"Maybe we should just throw Ethan into the fire?" Cameron mused.

"Not helpful, Cameron," Nathaniel gave her a dirty look.

"How about just putting the part of Ethan it is attached to in the fire?"

"Cameron!" The other three yelled at the same time.

"The portal is under the firepit, and I am not willing to accidentally send my friend to a world that has things like that!" Nathaniel was panicking. Ethan could die. They all could die if the creature used up Ethan and went after them. Nathaniel was sort of attached to his life. After a second, Nathaniel added, "Or set Ethan on fire, for that matter."

"The thought vampire has stayed attached to him. I wonder if there is a way to detach it? Belinay would know what to do," Cheshire said.

"Do you think like a human? Can you grab it and toss it in?" Cassandra was staring straight at an appalled Cheshire. "Oh, COME ON!" continued Cassandra. "I've seen what you really are."

Cheshire nodded, took a deep breath, and reached for the thought vampire. Cheshire's hand grabbed nothing. Not only did it seem that the thought vampire could not impact Cheshire, Cheshire could not impact the thought vampire.

Ethan moaned and his eyes closed.

"Can we take the fire to him?" This time, Cameron made some sense.

Cheshire reached into the firepit, and grabbed a burning branch. That was used to stab the thought vampire. Then with flick of the wrist, Cheshire tossed the creature into the firepit and watched it get sucked in. He turned to the other three, "DONE!"

"What is done?" Asked Ethan from the ground, but no one answered. "My butt hurts. I am thirsty." Then he got up and went into the building to grab drinks. A few minutes later he came out and handed everyone their drink.

Everyone opened their cans and stood staring into the fire for a few minutes.

Then, Nathaniel asked, "What was it we were talking about just now?"

No one remembered.

Bad Ghost, Good Ghost

Belinay was excited. In order to make sure that the thought vampire had jumped to Ethan, she had pushed herself away from it to one of the officers. And, for the first time, she managed to possess someone. Too bad it was someone that did not appreciate the power of bathing regularly. Belinay found she could just rest in him, and let him be himself. His living dynamism was recharging her. Later, when he got home, with considerable effort, Belinay made him take a shower. Then she left him. Then she jumped in again. Then she left him again. Oh, this was so much fun!

Alas, alas, she knew it was wrong to take over someone for no good reason. The officer seemed exhausted. Belinay felt more rested and animated than she had in ages. She had died seventeen years ago at the age of 106. At that age she had not exactly been dancing the cha-cha on a regular basis. It had taken her spirit months to learn to properly manifest. It took even longer to jump distances in manifestation. She had always felt sluggish. But now, she felt like a twenty-year-old without the nuisance of an actual body.

As she was about to jump to the campsite, she felt an odd presence in the house next door. Oh no. Then again, this was in the nearby town, so no worries it would impact the campsite. La-di-dah and off she went.

****

Playing with a Ouija board without understanding its possibilities was dumb. Yes, these were sold as toys. The name came from the French (oui) and German (ja) for "yes." Although, anyone with a bit of unknown power could accidentally use it as a centering. Centering objects can be used in meditation to focus on and clear the mind. The bad thing about the Ouija board was that the centering wasn't internal. It was external to whatever happened to be hanging out.

Even dumber was not putting the proper wards and restrictions before using the board. Even the simple phrase, "those with good intentions," would have helped. Ignorance was not bliss.

The dumbest thing they could have done? They used the board in a cemetery. Why, oh, why had he agreed to be a temporary camera guy for the incompetent amateur ghost hunters? Because he needed the money. The pandemic had just about killed his photography and video business and he was barely recovering. He should just get a real job. He wondered what someone with few skills could work at. Helping wannabe influencers was not the way to go. But then, they HAD paid in advance. They had paid a lot.

Now Alexandros had the dratted girl ghost, who had obviously been a spoiled brat while alive, in his house. He was sure it was the girl caught on his video, even though he had not actually seen her in the house. She had looked right at the camera and sneered. The ghost hunters were ecstatic at the footage. They had given him a bonus. Now he thought she had actually let him know she was attaching to him. Alexandros was not ecstatic.

If anything in the house was breakable, it could end up in pieces. If it was not breakable, it could end up flying anywhere. If something was needed, it was hidden. When a friend had visited, an attack happened. If he left out food, it was smeared on the nearest hard surface. If sleep was attempted, the screeching humming started. He had gone to a hotel and it happened there, too. The vibrations through the floor and the visions of the antique clock were particularly unnerving. Hauntings were a misery. The misery was worse because he had never before believed in ghosts.

The thought of running around town, yelling, while waving his hands in the air crossed his mind. At least, it would release some tension.

He thought about calling the same ghost hunters to help clear the house. Something tickled the back of his mind. Someone nearby knew about these things. Not a religious organization, though that could also be an option. Something rumored that had happened decades ago....

****

"Belinay! BELINAY! Bel-in-ay!" Cheshire was a bit happy and decided to show it. This was the friend that Cheshire had seen born and could still talk to as a ghost. Cheshire had the feeling that she had disappeared, possibly for good, but did not know why.

"You know, while I was out possessing a stinky police officer so he could take a shower, I noticed the house next to him seemed to have a yucky presence," Belinay tried to appear casual. As they all seemed fine, she chose not to mention the thought vampire.

Cassandra looked at her, her voice strained, "Is this related to the cycle?"

"You look a little stressed. Have you thought about using a deep hydration face cream?" Belinay joked.

"That would not really lower the stress," Cheshire commented.

"No, but it would make her look less stressed," continued Belinay.

"I am NOT stressed!" yelled Cassandra.

"It didn't feel like it's part of the cycle," said Belinay. "It seemed more *stubborn* than anything else. Unless we want to bring it the campsite. I would not stress about it, Cassandra. Where are the others by the way?"

"Nathaniel and Ethan are probably at their jobs. They seemed really worn out, especially Ethan. I am not sure why as it was only 10:30 when we got back. At their age, that was when my night started," Cassandra said. "I am on vacation today, which is why you get the privilege of my presence."

"So-o-o, what do you think it was?" Cheshire was excited. Not only was Belinay back, but suddenly there was something to do besides sit at a desk. Cheshire had not bothered to go to the office. It was not like getting fired was a worry.

"Typical child poltergeist. It felt young and tantrum-y, but mean rather than playful. I had never been in that area while dead before, so I am not sure how long it has been there. You know how an actual body prevents full sensing."

"Can we bring it to the firepit? Send it into the light, like in those silly haunting shows? I have never dealt with a human child ghost before!" Cheshire really wanted some action.

"NO! Thinking the cycle may be restarting is bad enough. Knowing what can happen at the site that Nathaniel and Ethan are now regularly taking people to, especially the children, is worse. NO! I do not think we should consider bringing a rotten little spirit there! Do you seriously want to ADD to the problems that happen there?" Cassandra was freaking out.

"Hmm. Stressing out will cause wrinkles," said Belinay. Cassandra would come around.

"More wrinkles," corrected Cheshire. Cassandra had not handled her fiftieth birthday with complete grace.

"I am not stressing about the campsite or Nathaniel." The looks they gave her let Cassandra know they were fully aware of her lie.

"Perhaps add in a lavender scrub?" Belinay suggested.

Cassandra blew out a breath and threw her apron on the counter. Then she walked away to sit on the couch and pretend that the TV held her interest.

"Can we? Please?" Cheshire was glowing with anticipation.

Belinay beamed.

****

Alexandros looked out the picture window and saw the most hideous vehicle pulling up in front of his house. He had just finished cleaning up his breakfast, and himself. The full cereal bowl had invisibly risen and been placed upside down on his head. He was eating out of the cereal box rather than risk a repeat. And he was hungry. His food kept getting destroyed or disappeared.

He had gone to a restaurant and felt the presence follow him. Food trays had been tipped, People had been tripped. Drinks had been pushed into laps. Thankfully, none of this happened close enough to him that he could get blamed. He was now afraid to leave the house because the invisible creature might follow him.

The color on that van should be illegal. The person coming to the door with the weird smile seemed familiar. He might as well greet his guest. He opened the door while shoving a handful of cereal into his mouth, "Mmm Ah hp yu?"

"Actually," Cheshire said. "I came to help you." Belinay had not allowed Alexandros to see her and was searching the house for the dead human imp.

Alexandros stared and stopped chewing. Then he started to cough as he choked on his mouthful. Once he caught his breath again, he said, "Who are you and why do you think I need your help? Whatever you are selling, I cannot afford it. And I am an atheist as of this moment."

"My name is Cheshire and I work in Token Village. Have you had issues with a spiritual being?"

"Found her! Got her! I think I can drag her downstairs!" Only Cheshire heard Belinay's shouts. Then, a series of thumps down the stairs, scrapes on the wall, things getting knocked over, and unearthly shrieks were heard. Alexandros cringed, several times, at the noise. Only Cheshire, though, could see Belinay struggling with the ghost child, like she was trying to hold a large hyped-up raccoon.

"Why would you think I have an issue with a spiritual being?" A pause filled with screeches.

"My name is Alexandros, by the way."

****

The ghost girl had been placed into a small cannister that had once held film. Cheshire had explained to Alexandros that spirits did not have mass, so they could be put into any size container. Once trapped, if the container was not opened, the spirit was stuck.

The cylinder was the smallest thing that Alexandros could find. It had taken both Belinay and Cheshire close to thirty minutes to get the ghost scalawag in there. Belinay had made herself visible to Alexandros and had scared the daylights out of him. She had compared the experience to sticking a mountain lion into a domestic cat's travel crate. The unholy sounds that the girl ghost had made had been accompanied by scratches all over Cheshire. These healed within minutes, but they did not make Cheshire happy. Objects had been pulled and thrown hard enough to break them. A thrown one had missed Alexandros's head by an inch. Once the rascal was confined, Alexandros had gleefully sealed the cannister with both superglue and duct tape.

The unrelenting cries from the ghoulish child could still be heard. The container had wiggled enough to make it hard to hold. It was wildly hurdling around the glove compartment in Alexandros's truck at the moment. He had insisted on driving because no way was he going to be seen in Cheshire's van. Throughout all of this, he was actually worried about what the neighbors would think of it parked in front of his house.

"Think you can find the grave?" Belinay asked. When his companions had told him what they were going to do with the container, he could only think that it was NOT something he wanted to do. Then he decided that after the last couple of weeks, it could not get worse. He would be so wrong on that.

Alexandros turned into the graveyard and parked where he had the night of the recording. The group went to the headstone where the ghost child had been recorded. The chiseled words were too faded to read the name or dates. "This one, I think," he said. What could happen if it was the wrong grave, anyway?

Cheshire dug a hole with his hands, and jammed the cylinder in there. He placed a brick on top of the cylinder. Then he filled in the hole and tamped the earth down. He looked up at Alexandros, "That should hold her."

Except that was the wrong final resting place. The ghost of the person buried there now had to deal with the wraith. It was, well, unhappy. And it had gotten a look at Alexandros and the truck he drove.

****

Alexandros had returned to his house and watched Cheshire and Belinay drive away. He had then hurried himself to a restaurant where he gorged on chicken-fried steak, mashed potatoes, buttered carrots, a dinner roll, salad, soup and two pieces of pie. He had to unbutton his pants while driving. He was grinning as he walked in the door of his house. He started to head up the stairs for a good long sleep when he saw it.

Sitting at the dining room table was the ghost of a man in clothing from decades ago. Alexandros knew it was a ghost because he could see right through him. The shade was rhythmically tapping a cannister against the table. Each tap prompted an outraged growl.

Alexandros fell to his knees and dropped his head in his hands. "I don't suppose you would be willing to wait until morning so I can get some rest?" At this point, the ghost turned out to be gentleman. It gave Alexandros a sympathetic look and a short nod. On the other hand, it was not like it had anything else to do.

Alexandros did not wait. He ran up the stairs, grateful he could not hear the growls from his bedroom, and promptly fell into a deep sleep. His second thought before nodding off was that he would have to make a trip to Token Village. His first was that he should have gone to the bathroom.

When Alexandros got up the next morning, the man ghost had resorted to rolling the cannister back and forth, tossing it in the air, and shaking it on occasion. The growls had turned into outright snarls. The man ghost seemed to be getting some odd sort of pleasure from it.

Alexandros made some coffee and served the male ghost a mug. The male ghost finally set the cannister down. He leaned over the cup of coffee and Alexandros swore the ghost inhaled the scent. The wistful look that came over the ghost's face let Alexandros know that caffeine had long been valued. The sounds from the cannister had subsided to whimpers.

Caffeinated and fed, dry cereal again, Alexandros looked at the ghost and asked, "Would you happen to know how to get to Token Village?"

The ghost's face lit up and he answered clearly, "Cheshire!"

****

Alexandros followed the directions of the ghost toward Token Village. He had been unable to locate it on a map, hence no GPS instructions. It occurred to him on the drive that these ghosts were not behaving per classical stories. They could interact with solid objects. They were not tied to one location. They could communicate intelligently. They looked pretty darn good considering how long they had been dead.

When he made the last turn going down the hill, he realized he had been there before. The General Store always had what he wanted when he had gone on some of his rambles. And filling up at the gas station gave him an unusual amount of mileage for a tankful. How could he have not realized what this place was?

Alexandros parked in front of the jail, and he and the ghost, who was visible to all, walked in. The ghost carried the cannister. As they entered, Cheshire jumped up and ran to the ghost, "Lockerton! What are you doing here?"

"Do you happen to know anything about this?" Lockerton said, waving the cannister around. The growls started up again. "It was placed in my grave for some reason. It sounds to me like a dratted girl that needs a good talking to. I am not sure how long I had been in the in-between resting, but her racket brought me back out. I would like to get back to that."

Embarrassed, Alexandros and Cheshire gave a rambling explanation of the ghost girl, with a considerable number of apologies. When they were finished, there was a sound from the other side of the room. Detective Nickel had heard the whole thing and was staring at them horrified. "I am going to be out the rest of the day with these gentlemen," said Cheshire. Detective Nickel simply nodded, wide-eyed.

****

Cassandra was enjoying her time alone. She was in her lounge-about clothes, singing and dancing to the radio. Vacation days so agreed with her. She might even take a shower later. She could have Belgian waffles and ice cream for dinner. Oh, she really liked THIS song. She stopped. Standing in the doorway were Cheshire, a male ghost, and some stranger.

Yeah, she was mortified.

"Any chance you could contact Belinay?" Cheshire asked, apparently unaware of her discomfort. The ghost was looking everywhere but at her. The stranger was obviously amused.

Cassandra told her guests to make themselves at home and excused herself. Twenty minutes later, appearing more likely to want to be seen by others she came back. She went to a cabinet and pulled out the Ouija board. The stranger looked dismayed. "That's what started this whole mess!" he claimed. Cassandra stared at him. He looked away, then looked back, then said, "Name is Alexandros."

Cassandra nodded, not bothering to introduce herself, placed the special rock on top of the Ouija board, and called out to Belinay. A few seconds later, there was Belinay. "Lockerton?" was the first thing she asked.

"Of course, you would be involved in this," Lockerton answered.

"You know each other?" Not that Cassandra was terribly surprised. Belinay had been around for a while, and this guy seemed to know Cheshire.

"Of course, we do. He's Ethan's great-great-uncle," confirmed Belinay, giving Lockerton a wink.

"I am the great-great-aunt," she told Alexandros. Alexandros did remember to close his gaping mouth.

"I thought you decided to rest like most humans." Belinay had turned back to Lockerton.

"I had."

Once again Cheshire and Alexandros told the rambling story, this time to Cassandra, with a few smart-aleck remarks by Belinay. The decision was made to go to the firepit to pull from its magic. This was a guest night at Nathaniel's Firepit, but really, why would Nathaniel and Ethan mind? They would all be out of there by evening, anyway.

Possibly.

****

Nathaniel looked around as he went down the evening checklist. Sitting area cleaned. Trash cans with new plastic bags. Trash barrel with lid latched. Tent areas raked and cleared of debris. Firepit circle cleaned, set up, and ready to be lit. Extra ....

Cheshire's squash-colored disaster was coming up the drive. Behind it, a truck followed. Nathaniel hoped the second was not a guest. The occupants of the first vehicle would make that guest run away. Then again, anyone that was willing to follow Cheshire's intriguing-colored van had courage. Ethan stepped out of the building.

"Hello! Welcome to Nathaniel's Firepit! This is not a good time. Please leave and come back when no guests are expected," Nathaniel cheerfully greeted them. He was ignored. The headache started as soon as he realized the truck held an unknown ghost along with the driver. WHAT was that sound coming from whatever the ghost held in his hand?

"I will need salt, a piece of string, and a paper plate," Belinay order Ethan. He obeyed. Everyone always obeyed Belinay, even though she had never been known to hurt anyone. He returned and gave Belinay her items, then walked away. She set the paper plate upside down, then filled the bottom edge with salt all the way around. This formed a containment circle, she hoped. Nathaniel looked on, incredibly annoyed that she would interrupt him right before guests would arrive.

"All right. All of you need to follow my instructions," she nodded in assurance.

"Destructions," muttered Cassandra and Lockerton at the same time.

"Oh, no, please, not now. Can't this wait until tomorrow?" Nathaniel begged. He was promptly ignored.

Belinay explained that human spirits went to a place she called the in-between. At that place they could fall into rest or come to terms with their life. These spirits could then go on to stay at rest or continue with whatever beliefs they held in life. Sometimes, spirits refused to go, and would get stuck on earth. The being confined to the cannister was one of those. They were going to force her to go. That failing, they would find a place to put the cannister where the mischief-maker couldn't bother anyone.

Belinay placed the cannister in the center of the paper plate. She had everyone form a circle around her and the plate while holding hands. No one seemed fazed that a ritual would get performed with a paper plate. Then she said some sort of incantation that no one understood while reaching into the salt circle and winding the string around the cannister. The reverberations inside the cannister became almost unbearable.

"Repeat after me. You need to concentrate on that cannister and getting what is inside to the in-between," Belinay said. Then she proceeded to state more incantations which they all dutifully repeated. This was repeated several times.

Slowly, the noises coming from the cannister began to fade. Then, one particularly long howl emerged from it. Silence. Belinay continued with the words, and the rest repeating them. The cannister also faded and disappeared. Belinay carefully lifted the plate, making sure not to spill any salt. She placed the plate into the center of the firepit where it would burn when the fire was lit.

The girl's ghost had made it to the in-between. Well, that was the theory at least. Spirits could be woken up, but the girl's spirit was bound in the cannister while there, so she could not escape. Nathaniel hoped that the other spirits there would be able to rest with her around. He also hoped that no guest would question a plateful of salt in the middle of his firepit.

"What was it that you had us saying? And how did you know this would work?" Nathaniel wanted to know.

"Not an Earth language nor ritual," confirmed Belinay. "I needed something non-rhythmic to force all of you to focus your feelings on that cannister. And I am so glad that it DID work. I was struggling to remember it." She floated away leaving Nathaniel with an exasperated look toward the sky and mumbling about why he was expected to deal with these things. All he wanted was to have a business that could run without strange problems. Was that too much to ask?

In the meantime, Lockerton smiled at Belinay, gently stroked her cheek, and faded out. He had returned to his rest. Belinay winked out soon after. Cheshire and Alexandros loaded themselves into their respective vehicles and drove off. Cassandra had decided to stay for the evening.

****

Nathaniel looked toward the edge of the camp as he went to finish the checklist. At the edge stood a young boy, of about the age when children stop seeing the unknown. He looked over and realized that a tent had been set up. Apparently, Ethan had continued to take care of guests while Nathaniel went through that ridiculous rite. He could not tell if the boy was apprehensive or excited or simply awed. If that boy had seen the circle and heard the nonsense chanting, there would be some interesting conversations in his future. Suddenly, Nathaniel knew what story he would be telling tonight. Hopefully, he could calm any fear the child had.

He glanced over and saw that Ethan was helping to set up a tent. The other guests would be arriving soon. For tonight, everything would be fine. Nathaniel went back to the camp building and started pulling out the food and drinks. Really, this ghost stuff was not as bad as his mother had feared.

That became the moment that Nathaniel would remember as having tempted fate.

A Lot of Fur

Throughout history, people have used their imaginations to find an explanation for things they cannot comprehend. As the explanations get passed around, they can take on a life of their own. Fancies about creatures can become reality for some. There are a lot of beings that people claim to have seen or found proof on. Scientists, as well as most other completely sane people, disagree with the findings.

In Lake Champlain, between New York and Vermont, there is a supposed lake monster. It has been named Champ, or Gitaskog in the Abenaki language. It is described as a large horned serpent, and a very fast swimmer. Sightings have occurred for hundreds of years. Recently, the sightings have reached into the dozens in a year. If scientists ever manage to get DNA from both, they will find that Gitaskog is a fifth cousin, twice-removed, of Nessie of Loch Ness.

The jackalope first appeared in 1934 in Douglas, Wyoming. It is a rabbit or hare, usually white, with horns or antlers. It can also "sing like a fine tenor," although no verified recordings exist. No one has explained why a person would want to listen to one sing, either. There is no good reason why a rabbit or hare would need horns. Nor, as far as anyone knows, have any deer filed a claim against missing antlers. Somehow, specimens and postcards keep showing up in tourist shops, though no one sees them in the wild.

Bigfoot got its name when giant footprints were found by loggers in the Northwest United States in the 1950s. Bigfoot has extended its range to now be seen in pretty much every forest in the United States and Canada. In the last few decades, Bigfoot has become very popular with mockumentaries, articles, and supposed pictures. Videos now abound as well. Bigfoot is described as a tall, hairy thing that looks like a man or an ape with long arms. Apparently, you can smell a Bigfoot, but never see it, except from afar while it throws boulders.

The nocturnal mountain snipe is a little black weasel-like creature with cream colored paws, and dark red nose. Its large brown eyes are perfectly round, making it look almost like an animated character. It weighs about a pound and LOVES peanut butter. It is attracted to the sound of paper bags. Young children are encouraged to lure them and feed them on night hunts. They are fairly gentle, but if bitten by one, you get itchy on the bottoms of your feet. This is mostly because they are too small to bite any higher than a person's ankle.

A Scotsman tried to breed Wild Haggis in America's Rocky Mountains. It did not work. These critters have legs on one side longer than the other so they can travel on the steep sides of Scottish mountains. But with one side with longer legs, they can only go in one direction on a mountain. Otherwise, they topple over, and the Scotsman spent too much time picking them up. That, and mountain lions found them to be kind of tasty.

So many critters ....

****

Chaos. That was the only word that Nathaniel could come up with. The last of the food had been devoured by the smelly beast with a few disgusting bits still laying on the ground. The guests that had run screaming all over the place had scared the beast. The beast had reacted by trying to tear the tents apart. Most of the tents had collapsed from the beast's battering, but no overall damage happened to them. Despite the rule against food in the tents, the beast had found stashes and devoured those as well. Nathaniel hoped it got a tummy ache.

The guests were now huddled around the firepit. They had come down from the trees, from behind the building, from under a table. Some looked visibly stunned. At least this had happened in the early evening, and not the dead of night. "Dead" was probably not a good choice of wording.

Ethan had managed to get the tents that had fallen back up with help from the guests. No one had been physically injured. Several guests were a bit excited, actually. A few were looking at videos on their phones that they took during the attack instead of seeking shelter. No one was allowed to leave until the authorities, or rather, Detective Nickel, arrived. Nathaniel hoped that Cheshire came as well. Cheshire would know what to do.

"Guess we will have to offer a refund," moaned Ethan. Always thinking ahead, was Ethan.

Nathaniel saw Detective Nickel drive up. He breathed a sigh of relief when he noticed that Cheshire was with him. Cheshire went directly into the building without looking at anyone. Detective Nickel swaggered up to Nathaniel, "So what exactly happened here?"

Nathaniel took a deep breath because he knew he would sound nuts. "We had a Bigfoot attack."

Detective Nickel blinked, "It doesn't look like it was a terrible attack. Is everyone all right? I assume you would have had the idea to call an ambulance if they weren't. But never assume. And you meant 'bear" right?"

"No one was physically injured. We cleaned up the campsite. And when you start asking people, you will see that I really did mean 'Bigfoot.' There aren't any bears that big in this area. The few black bears that might be around are not likely to come into a large group of people, especially with a fire going."

Detective Nickel gave Nathaniel a disgusted look, "No big bears in the area. But there are Bigfoots? Uh, Bigfeet? A Bigfoot! And then you cleaned up a crime scene?"

"Animals cannot commit a crime, so there cannot be a crime scene. No one was injured, so there was no reason to not set things straight."

"So, an animal and not a non-existent creature? Can't keep your story straight, can you?" Detective Nickel could be a jerk.

"Bigfoot, now that it appears to exist, would be an animal. Maybe you should just do your job and get the information you need," Nathaniel wasn't in the mood to deal with him.

Detective Nickel plodded off to talk to the guests. After a few statements and watching a few phone videos, he seemed agitated. Nathaniel felt a little bad for him, as he knew it would be beyond his abilities to follow up. Nickel stomped back and stated, "It is not my job to investigate animal incidents. Put together a list of the clients and their contact information. I will let the Fish and Wildlife Service know that they need to get up here." On second thought, Nathaniel did not feel the least bit bad for the detective.

Detective Nickel trudged back to his car and drove off without Cheshire. So, Nathaniel went in hunt of Cheshire. He found Cheshire still in the building calmly using the computer. How Cheshire always managed to get into password-protected technology was beyond him. The printer whirred and there was the guest list.

"I suppose you have an idea what to do about this creature?" Nathaniel asked Cheshire.

Cheshire nodded, "It found food here once, so it will be back. Bigfoot should be extinct, but occasionally one time-jumps because of the firepit."

"Wait! You are saying these things were real once?! Why cannot they not stay as a myth?"

"There are many animals that have traveled between and lived on two or more continents: wolves, cats, camels, even pre-historic horses. Why not some ancient, giant, orange-haired ape? But they died out tens of thousands of years ago. Apes live in forest areas. When an animal dies in forest areas, most remains will get eaten and scattered. The few scattered fossils that might, maybe, have survived would be what led to the legends."

"Wait! You said the firepit is also a time machine! Is there no end to this? And how do you know about Bigfoot? And, and, and, why me?"

"Because you decided to open the campsite. You restarted the firepit even after getting warned by your mother. I have lived a very long time and seen many things. As an extra-terrestrial, I can also time-jump using the firepit. I have traveled to different times and seen these in person. That means I can help you. It was hungry and scared, but that does not make it less dangerous. By the way, the portal is naturally occurring, and not a machine."

"You are an extra-terrestrial. Of course, why should I be surprised about anything right now?" Nathaniel was losing it.

"Again, I also know how to send it back to its own time period. Are you stressed or something? You are acting weird." Cheshire was concerned. Nathaniel just sat on the ground and covered his face with his hands.

Ethan came out of the building and said, "I am going down to the General Store to get more supplies. I am getting hungry."

At least some things stay the same, thought Nathaniel.

"Ethan, give me a ride to the jail," Cheshire called out. "I will be back later," Cheshire said to Nathaniel.

Nathaniel was still sitting on the ground as he watched Ethan and Cheshire drive away. He glanced back at the tents and the guests. He had responsibility for all of them. With the attack, he had already failed them once. He peered into the nearby woods remembering Cheshire's warning about the Bigfoot returning. It also occurred to him that the Bigfoot may have been coming to the campsite when no one was there.

Nathaniel felt very much alone.

****

Cheshire's vegetal chaos-colored van parked in front of Cassandra's house. Ethan had returned to the campsite with a truck full of food. Cheshire sincerely hoped that the Bigfoot would wait before also returning. Nathaniel could be alone up there with only Ethan for help, though some of the guests might be available.

Cassandra gave him an incensed look. She knew it could not be anything good. She stepped back inside and by the time Cheshire had settled down, Belinay had arrived.

"Bigfoot is actually kind of cool," Cassandra admitted after hearing the story.

"He can tear you into little pieces and then munch on your body parts," Belinay reminded her. Cassandra didn't look worried. Apes were not, in general, meat-eaters, and generally only attacked in self-defense or fear.

"I wouldn't worry about Fish and Wildlife," Belinay continued to Cheshire. "I seriously doubt they will make it there any time soon. They are more likely to look for 80-something-year-old men fishing without a license."

"Well, then, let's head to the firepit," Cheshire said. And the cavalry set off to the rescue. Hopefully, there WOULD be a rescue.

****

Nathaniel had convinced the majority of the guests to just go away. Most of them had not needed any prodding, but started packing as soon as Detective Nickel drove away. Ethan looked frustrated at tearing down tents he had just finished re-setting up. Nathaniel did help as well, though he kept getting distracted by the nearby woods. He offered refunds, but only one couple took it. The others probably thought it was better than any story he could tell them. He suspected those with videos thought they would make money off of the them. Then there was the fellow who refused to budge. That fellow stated that at the age of 78, gosh-durn-it, he was not about to leave without getting a good night's rest. Apparently, 78-year-olds can sleep with a Bigfoot around.

The van coming up the drive filled him with such an intense relief that he felt giddy. Nathaniel just wanted this weekend to be over, so he could return to his repetitive desk job. Ethan was cooking dinner, so at least they would all get to eat before confronting Bigfoot. That was providing Bigfoot did not decide to become a dinner guest. The older fellow was giving Ethan unsolicited advice.

During dinner, the group came up with a plan while the old man picked out a cot and went to sleep. Because of the danger, Cassandra, Nathaniel, Ethan, and the older fellow would stay inside the building. Belinay would try to lure Bigfoot back to the firepit. Cheshire would then shapeshift to his extra-terrestrial form and make sure the beast would time-jump back to its proper era.

"Shapeshifter? This is not your real look?" Nathaniel was agog.

"Obviously," Cheshire gave Nathaniel a look. "You don't really suppose that extra-terrestrials only have human characteristics? Right?" Nathaniel knew better than to answer.

"The thing is," said Nathaniel staring down at his hands, "that I will need a lot of therapy. BUT, I cannot discuss this in therapy. I would end up with the kind of therapy that I do not need."

Belinay laughed. Then she winked out as she set off to search for the ape. It took about three hours, and the others were nodding off in the building by that time. The older fellow was sound asleep on a cot snoring like a moose looking for a mate. The thrashing would have alerted them. Belinay yelling, "I am a-coming! Roaring down this-here mountain!" gave more notice. Everyone ran to the window to look.

When the two clattered into the firepit clearing, Belinay ceased to be visible. Nathaniel actually snickered at the look of bafflement on Bigfoot.

Cheshire ran out the door, and transformed into a hummingbird. Now, Cheshire's species of hummingbirds are about ten inches in length, can travel up to 60 miles an hour, and have a wasp-like stinger. Even though, like Earthly hummingbirds, Cheshire's folks can fly in any direction, they are very careful when going backwards. At those speeds, their stinger will stick like a push pin into anything they run into. Cheshire would now also camouflage perfectly with the van.

Cassandra and Nathaniel pushed up against the window pane to watch. They looked at each other, apprehension mirrored in their eyes. Ethan stared at his phone. Nathaniel sincerely hoped the older fellow's snorting was not attractive to Bigfoot.

Outside, Cheshire was zipping around Bigfoot's face. Bigfoot moved his head around trying to keep Cheshire in his sight. Oddly, Bigfoot seemed too mesmerized by Cheshire to swat. Then Cheshire would hover in front of Bigfoot, and zip slightly backward. At which point, Bigfoot would take a couple of steps towards the firepit. This continued on and on and on. Then continued some more.

When Bigfoot came close enough to the fire, an energetic feeling filled the air. Buzzing was felt throughout their bodies. A ringing noise seemed to be coming from everywhere all at once. Cassandra hugged herself and shivered. Nathaniel decided it would not be a good time to throw up.

Nathaniel saw the trees behind the firepit change. There was an overlap of two different forests. He had the feeling of age and coolness when he looked at the new overlap. One tree shimmered where the overlap had a tree in the same spot as the present.

Suddenly Cheshire zipped to the edge of the trees, and Bigfoot followed. Bigfoot crashed into the overlap and slowly both faded away. Now, only the present forest could be seen. Nathaniel and Cassandra felt a loss without the buzzing and ringing.

Cheshire appeared back at the fire and circled it a few times. Then Cheshire transformed back to human form, went to the van, and drove away. Nathaniel and Cassandra could only stare. At that point, they realized they should have closed the door after Cheshire ran out.

"Hey," said Ethan looking up from his phone. "Did you know that male orangutans can make a noise that can be heard a mile away?"

The older fellow slept on.

****

The Fish and Wildlife Service had done a very superficial investigation. No injuries had happened. It was a supposedly mythical creature. Nothing could be found of said creature, except for a few footprints. Those footprints were smudged by all the running around of the guests. It could possibly be a hoax drummed up by an influencer. They were lucky that no one had gotten hurt in what must have been a prank. Nathaniel briefly wondered how animal attack investigations were actually done. Then he decided he never wanted to find out.

Nathaniel was surprised by the increase in traffic to the website. Apparently, the Bigfoot videos posted all over social media, along with news sites, had created a lot of publicity. The whackaloons who strived to find these types of things wanted to come see for themselves. Nathaniel would never publicly admit what had happened in those videos. Yup, he would only reference Fish and Wildlife's findings. He kind of liked having this type of secret.

He had put a notice both on the website and in the Terms and Conditions that there was no guarantee that something unusual or supernatural could EVER happen. Then re-emphasized that Nathaniel's Firepit was ONLY a family-friendly campsite. Fifty percent of spaces would be reserved for families. No refunds would be offered for anything out of the ordinary.

Nathaniel was no longer sure what he considered ordinary. He wondered if he could even be amazed.

Rectangular Block

"That's pretty amazing," said Nathaniel. He was staring at the rectangular structure that had shown up sometime in the last week next to the grill at the campsite. He was pretty sure that it was a joke, like the ones in California and Wales. Or not, considering what the fire was. Hopefully it was not some sort of weapon. He realized that he would have to deal with this before the first guests started to arrive.

The intensity of the structure's black color absorbed light to the point the immediate area around it looked distorted. It was not very large. He could see over the top. He probably could have wrapped his arms around it. He was not about to touch it until the backup arrived, if backup said he could. He had done what many adults in their mid-twenties did when something out of his realm of knowledge occurred. He had called his mom.

"WHAT is that?" Nathaniel jumped a foot off the ground at Ethan's shout directly behind him.

"A monolith."

"A mano-what?"

"M-o-n-o-l-i-t-h." Nathaniel spelled it twice more before Ethan got it in his phone for searching.

"It doesn't look like it is made of stone," he then stated.

"Well, what else would we call it?" Nathaniel did not expect an answer. Ethan shrugged and headed back to the truck to start unloading for the weekend. Nathaniel made to follow, but gave it a backward glance first. He stopped a few steps later. Did that thing actually WINK at him?

****

"Never seen anything like it," said Cassandra.

"No earthly idea what it is," said Belinay.

"I do not know," said Cheshire.

"How would a monolith get here?" asked Nathaniel.

"It's not made of stone."

"So, what is it called?" Nathaniel asked. This conversation had already happened.

"Monolith will work."

There it was again. In the center of the upper third, what looked like two little gray circles appeared. Then one of them flattened to a half-circle arc before returning to a circle. It was WINKING. Or it was resetting for something truly dire. Or it was a trick of the light. Or it was some kind of portal. Then both circles went away. Nathaniel felt like just ignoring it and continuing with the campsite setup. Guests would notice this, though.

"That little circle thing? Do you think that is good or bad?" asked Cassandra.

The others just looked at her. It was not something that could be explained right now. Monoliths in literature rarely had positive outcomes. Mysterious dark objects that winked at you were also not known for happy endings. Anything that showed up at random by a magical firepit seemed a little chilling.

"If it has eyes, maybe we can communicate with it?" Cheshire always seemed so willing to talk to strange beings, being strange as well.

"I think we need to do some research," Nathaniel decided. "Tomorrow. As long as it doesn't explode or begin shooting death rays or sucking guests into itself or ask me to take it to my leader or cause some weird disease in humans or expand to crush things around it or . . . ."

"We get it!" Cassandra was jittery. "As long as it doesn't do anything that would get you sued, then what? Seriously! Get to the point already!"

"It can stay there and I will call it part of the outdoor scheme. I will just make sure that no guests touch it." Nathaniel finished up. "I will go to the library tomorrow and see what I can find."

"What leader would we take it to in this situation?" Ethan asked.

****

"Please do not get too close to the monolith. It may be a little unstable," Nathaniel decided not to mention that unstable also meant not quite sane.

"What is it made from? It doesn't look like it is a rock," The woman looked like a grandmother. She certainly did not seem young enough for the four-year-old twins that had caused havoc tonight.

"Um, it's an alloy of some sort," Nathaniel decided that sounded logical.

"It shouldn't be called a monolith if it is not made of stone."

Did absolutely everyone on the planet know this? Nathaniel managed a grin without rolling his eyes, "That is what we are calling it until we can find a cutesy name for it."

"Huh." The woman walked away.

Nathaniel was glad they had only one guest night this weekend. He wasn't sure he could have dealt with the usual two. He had limited it to one night for a few weeks after the Bigfoot incident.

Throughout the evening, the monolith had shown its circles. The guests had been either curious, amused, or scared. These circles had not winked again, but moved all over as if watching. It had apparently distracted some of the guests to the point they forgot the food in their hands. Others seemed nervous and had retreated to their tents. Ethan had stood quite close to it and at one point looked incredibly startled towards it.

Nothing dreadful had happened this evening. Nathaniel decided to go to bed and deal with it in the morning after the guests had departed. Surely, he could find something at the library to help. Cassandra and Cheshire had mingled among the guests, but their wariness could be felt.

****

After Nathaniel and Ethan had cleaned up the campsite, Nathaniel had taken the drive to the nearest library. Two hours on the internet had yielded only information from fiction and outrageous claims about monoliths. Scholarly works were focused on archeology and geology. The first might not be too outrageous considering the one at the magical firepit. The second was fascinating, but not helpful in this case.

The look the librarian gave Nathaniel made him reconsider the phrasing *big stones that cause lots of destruction.* "I meant, the mythological consequences that occur with monoliths. Especially those that are not made of stone."

"Mono comes from the word for single. Lith comes from the word for stone. If it is not made from stone, it is not a monolith," the librarian stated with a wink.

Here we go again. "Then, if it isn't stone, what is it called?" Nathaniel asked with as innocent a look as he could muster.

Apparently, the librarian did not know either. "Why exactly do you need this?"

"Researching for a story?"

"You made that a question. A story?" The librarian was sincerely interested.

"Can you help me with information that I would not find after two hours of internet searching?" Nathaniel decided not to elaborate past that.

"Have you tried the books in our collection?"

This got a startled laugh out of Nathaniel, "That should have crossed my mind. What sections would I go to?"

The librarian gave him a list of possible areas. He found myths, history, paranormal, different countries, and religion. He had never known that Dewey's non-fiction system had a fiction section: 813.54. A separate list had authors who had written fiction about rocks or myths. The third page was a print-out of the searches from the library site. Nathaniel smiled.

He checked out several books to take back to the campsite. The others were still there after the guests had departed. He did not expect any of them to find anything new in the books.

It occurred to Nathaniel that he was getting a bit too used to these events.

****

The group had spent all afternoon and evening poring through the books. Everything was speculation in them. Which was exactly what they had expected. Nathaniel gave up and took the books back to his car. When he walked back to the building, there were several circles on the surface. All of them seemed to track his movement. Eventually, they all settled down for the night in the building, except for Belinay, who had decided to keep watch for the group.

The next morning, the monolith was twice as tall and it had moved to a different place. It was directly in front of the building door to be precise. At least it left enough room to creep around it without having to touch it. He used the back door, anyway. Nathaniel was freaking out. The circles continued following his progress. As the others emerged from the building, from the back door, it became obvious none of them were thrilled. And more circles had appeared.

Belinay, Cassandra, and Cheshire had sat at the breakfast table trying to brainstorm. They came up with exactly zero. Without really knowing what that thing was, or what it was doing, they couldn't know if it was dangerous. It did not give off good vibes. It took a bit to realize the monolith had moved again, this time closer to the building. They all considered staying in the cars overnight. Or better yet, go home. But they could not, in good conscious, leave the campsite. Then they realized they were all worried it would move on top of them and crush them. They decided to go home after all, and went into the building to gather their things. When they came out, the monolith was blocking the road, and there was no getting around it. They were going to spend the night in the building.

****

Pain. It felt like Ethan, Cassandra, and Nathaniel's heads would soon implode. Agony. It had reached the point that they all wished to pass out. Cheshire just seemed disoriented. Belinay was fine, and trying to find ways to ease the pain.

It had started when they were all within the building again. A scraping noise was heard. They had all looked up startled to see the monolith blocking the door. It had expanded to block the front window as well. It had wrapped itself around the building and blocked the back door and the other two windows. Not only was it now pitch-black inside, any light was getting absorbed by it.

They had discussed the levels of oxygen in the building, though that seemed fine so far. The vents in the small attic must not be blocked. Would they be able to tell if they started to need more oxygen? Belinay had thought she was unaffected, then found she could not leave the building. Whatever that thing was, it effectively blocked her movement. She was the only one who could see in the darkness, and it was not good. Then they had started to feel the headaches.

Belinay felt fear for the first time since she had died. What if it decided to crush the building? She did not want her friends to die. Cheshire's species were not capable of becoming ghosts. Cheshire was sprawled out, unresponsive. The others had reached the point of becoming dysfunctional. Nathaniel was quietly sobbing. Cassandra simply shook her head back and forth and moaned. Ethan had curled up into the fetal position. The suffering was wearing on Belinay. She had no idea what to do.

Suddenly, Cassandra screamed out, "STOP! PLEASE! JUST STOP! I CAN'T! I CAN'T! I CANNOT TAKE ANY MORE! Why do you want to hurt me like this? Whatever did I do to you?" The questions were whispered. Belinay went to her and hugged her close. Time passed. Slowly.

Belinay did not know how long she had sat and held Cassandra. The small amount of light in the building had not caught her attention until now. Part of it was the ability to see in the dark. But a larger part was that the increase had been very gradual. The bottom of one of the side windows showed a sliver of moonlight. Belinay carefully moved away from Cassandra and went to the window. She pushed up the bottom portion. A breeze floated in. In a few minutes, the entire window was unblocked.

Belinay started going around trying to get everyone to MOVE. "Come on. Come on. We have to get out the window while we can. Please, please, try." When that did not work, she started with Cheshire, and dragged him out. It would not have been pleasant, but he would heal from the scrapes and bruises. Once she had him outside, she noticed the back door was now unblocked.

She went back inside through the door, and grabbed Nathaniel next. She was halfway to the door, when Cheshire came up and said, "Want some help?" She gave a grateful look. Ethan was next. Belinay had decided to take them out of the building according to age. That, and Cassandra had more magical ability than the men. It was much easier with Cheshire's help, though he seemed to falter when he was inside.

When all of them were outside, they soon recovered. The pain was just gone. When they looked back, the entire building was covered by the monolith, which looked more like a blob now. It was not as dark as before, absorbing less light from around itself. All of them were wondering whether the building would survive. The circles watching them were disturbing.

"Does our insurance cover this?" wondered Ethan. He was ignored.

"Let's go home," said Cassandra. "We are not going to win this one."

****

All of them, sitting in Cassandra's living room, were honest enough to admit they had worried the monolith would be there when they arrived. They all kept glancing out the windows expecting the darkness to take over the house. No one voiced the fear that there might be more than one of those things out there.

Nathaniel remembered something about Ethan. "When you were standing near the monolith when we had guests, you looked like it had startled you. What happened?"

"It felt like someone had nudged me. Except not physically. More like my mind made me feel that someone was touching me, when no one was. Does that make sense?" Blank looks from the others all around. "You know," Ethan continued, "like when you think someone is watching you, but you know there is no one there. Except it was touching instead of feeling."

"Could it be trying to communicate through our brains?" Cheshire had to ask. "It would certainly explain the headaches you Earthlings had. Belinay wasn't affected because she no longer has a physical brain. And the effect was less on me because my species is wired differently than Earthlings. But if it is alive, it has to have something that functions like what we know as a brain. I bet it uses telepathy."

"It did not feel like communication. It felt like devastation. If it communicates that way, then we are all in trouble. And it was growing. Who knows how many people it can impact?" Cassandra paused. "Would it know that it cannot effectively communicate that way?"

"Do you think it would understand to listen actively and ask questions? Though I suppose telling us its plan would be nice." The sarcasm came from Belinay's frustration. The frustration did not allow her to be nice, but she did have a point. This was her fourth cycle, and she had never encountered something like this. Of course, everyone had heard of monoliths, and places like Stonehenge. THOSE did not move and cause people to scream out in anguish. Unless ….

"I think it is becoming a rock," Belinay explained. Cheshire looked at her as if she had lost her not-physical mind. Cassandra and Nathaniel passed a look that spoke volumes between the mother and son. Ethan started to smile.

"It wasn't as black when we left as when we first saw it! It could be, like, transforming!" Ethan exclaimed. "That is what you mean." Belinay beamed at him. That was exactly what she meant.

"Um, sure, ok, I mean, how long would that take?" asked Nathaniel. "And, not to be too fussy, but it is currently, at least I almost hope it still is, wrapped around a building. I do not want to think about jackhammering the building out of a boulder that just appeared. If a building is left under there. And, and, that's not even the beginning. How would we explain this? …. My stomach hurts from thinking about this." At least he and Ethan had a few days before the next guest day, so they would have time to re-organize, or cancel. *NOT good. Not good at all.* He thought.

"He learned to stress from you," Cheshire told Cassandra. She gave him an exasperated look.

"Have we agreed that this thing is alive?" asked Belinay. If she were not a ghost, that would have caused her to shudder. "If the headaches were an example of its communication, there is no way to stop it. None of the living can understand it without shocking themselves. I cannot even begin to connect."

"On the other hand, it allowed all of us to get out after you screamed," Belinay pointed out. "It may not have been communicating in a manner we understand. It did understand that it should not continue."

The group sat in the living room for a long time. Ideas were thrown out and discarded. The biggest problems they faced were not knowing whether it was alive or what it was. Without those two pieces of information, they could not formulate a plan. Maybe, if it was turning into a rock, they could do something. However, they did not know what was happening. They also weren't sure if it was growing or simply stretching. With so many unknown variables, they just wanted to sit in the living room and pretend nothing happened.

Although, eventually, they did come up with a plan. The plan would work if the building was still entombed. If not, then there might be a problem. And if the monolith was no longer there at all? They would have to decide whether to just move on with their lives, or hunt it down. It had to be tonight because Ethan, Nathaniel, Cassandra and Cheshire were all expected at work the next day.

****

The building was no longer enclosed by the monolith. The monolith was nowhere in sight, for that matter. The group inspected the site and everything seemed to be exactly as it should. Ethan noticed a slight track in the dirt, which led to broken branches at the edge of the woods. They had to make a decision. Should they follow the track or should they drive away and pretend this never happened? In the end, they acted like responsible adults and followed the track.

The track deepened as it went, almost as if the monolith was tiring and dragging itself. No tracks had been found in the campsite before, which meant that the monolith had been able to move without leaving a trail. As they progressed, the foliage showed more and more damage. It started with a few fragmented twigs and scattered leaves. Then they saw broken branches on larger plants and trees. Finally, a completely uprooted tree they had to skirt around. In a small clearing, they found the monolith. It was now a dark grayish color, sitting in the middle of the clearing, and shaped like a perfect cube.

"All right-y, we can leave it here. It's away from any hiking trails, and seems to be perfectly at ease. It has left the campsite and is on its way," Cheshire had lost interest in the thing as it did not seem any fun anymore. "Let's go."

Cheshire had just finished speaking when a hammering sound emerged from the block. Then it started to crunch. Cracks began to show as it transformed into a sphere. Bright white light appeared in the cracks. The light did not disperse outside of the sphere giving it a mesmerizing glow. The hammering sound increased. The group could feel it emanating through the ground and up their bodies until they felt themselves vibrating. Belinay was glowing in time to the oscillation. The inner light became brighter, then went out to utter darkness. The hammering noise stopped and the clearing was filled with silence. The group could hear only their own expectant breathing.

"Oh, jeez, it's gonna blow!" Ethan's eyes were wide as he reached this realization. That got a reaction.

They all scrambled behind trees not knowing if trees would provide any protection. They hunched down, closed their eyes, and covered their ears. Except for Belinay, who stayed put while staring open-mouthed. She would later describe the event.

It was not exactly a flash of light. The monolith had been digesting the light in order to slowly degrade into stone. Nor was it exactly an explosion, as it was controlled into a very definite area. It was not loud. Other than the pattering of some gravel onto the dirt, the noise simply did not happen. And yet, the group had the feeling of a colossal release of energy.

The result was an area filled with rocks and boulders in a somewhat circular manner. Some off-white rings were found looking a lot like the circles that had seemed to watch them. Cheshire tentatively tried to pick one up. It dissolved into ash. A geologist could probably classify the rocks and boulders, but no one in the group cared. They realized that the monolith had not meant any harm. It may not have had the capacity to understand what harm means. Wherever it had come from, it had completed its purpose. It had come to the area to die.

****

"I can't believe the monolith was alive," said Nathaniel, as he kicked back at a picnic table this fine Monday morning with a HUGE mug full of black coffee. He and Ethan had called off work. Cheshire had not even bothered since Detective Nickel would not care. Cassandra had left early, grumpy and mumbling. She was not an effective employee that day. The sheer mental effort of dealing with the thing had worn all of them out. They had decided to stay at the campsite. Even the thought of it coming back had not stopped them from sleeping all night. Thankfully, none of them had nightmares from the experience. Belinay had gone to rest in the in-between for a few hours and had just manifested again.

"Still was not originally a stone, and if it was alive, monolith is not the right word for it," said Cheshire. At this point, it was only about contradicting Nathaniel. That was rather fun. Quite frankly, Cheshire didn't care what it was called, so long as it stayed a scattered mess.

"Cheshire's right. Monolith would be a lifeless stone, and that seems kind of rude. We should think of something else," Belinay concurred. She grinned at Nathaniel's expression.

"Rude? It could have killed us! It could have destroyed the building! Had that been a true explosion, it could have wiped out a large area of the forest with us in it!" Nathaniel took a deep breath. He'd had enough. "Well, what are we going to call it?" This was getting redundant. They gave blank looks to each other. Monolith was the word they had started with, and now none of them could begin to come up with a different term.

A freshly showered, dressed, and breakfasted Ethan stepped out of the building. A look of surprise crossed his face at the looks everyone gave him. He looked around the campsite, then said, "I am glad the pillar transformed to rocks. And that it did it over there." He pointed. "I did not like that thing."

Pillar.

Action Figure

Cassandra was twelve-years-old when she watched the movie *Poltergeist* at a sleep-over party. She did not think it impacted her that much. Although, for a couple of years afterward, she struggled to be in a room by herself with a toy clown. That struggle included the Jack-in-the-Box her grandmother had in the toy corner behind the armchair at her house. Cassandra had adored that toy as a little tyke, and sometimes wondered what had happened to it.

Later, she had been gifted a ceramic clown by an acquaintance with bad taste. Not knowing what else to do with it, the clown was placed in the back of a high and out-of-the-way shelf. By that point, Cassandra was no longer afraid of clowns, toy or otherwise. Or so she told herself every time she took the clown and turned it to face the wall. Belinay would prank her by turning the clown back to face forward.

Cassandra would soon develop the same uneasy feelings about discount store action figures. Nathaniel and Ethan would come along with her.

****

The doll was sitting in the middle of the table when Nathaniel and Ethan walked into the building. It was one of those inexpensive action figures found at discount stores. The three-inch plastic form had painted eyes that were not quite centered. The paint used for the clothing would never be considered high quality. The joints looked like they would come apart at any moment. The boots, surprisingly, were muddy. Ethan picked up the action figure, shrugged, and tossed it into the lost and found.

The doll was standing cross-armed in the middle of the table when Nathaniel and Ethan came back with the last load from the truck. It startled them a wee bit. At least, it seemed like the same doll, only it was about a half-inch bigger. The eyes were now centered properly and had turned a bright blue reminiscent of a cop's flashing lights. The eyes MAY actually have been flashing. Nathaniel grabbed a kitchen towel, walked guardedly toward the table, and wrapped the action figure in it. Then he tossed it into the lost and found.

The doll, definitely bigger now, standing about five inches, was positioned in the middle of the table, leaning on a plastic knife when Nathaniel and Ethan came back from the campsite setup. The kitchen towel was nowhere to be seen. Ethan went to the lost and found and pulled out the towel. Then he stood there holding it out to Nathaniel. The silent battle of the wills lasted for close to a minute. Neither of them wanted to touch it. Finally, Nathaniel sighed, took the towel and approached the table. The action figure took the knife and lunged at Nathaniel. Nathaniel screamed. Ethan ran across the room to stand behind a pole.

It only took them a couple of seconds to realize it held a plastic knife. And that the action figure was only five inches tall. They both sprang at the doll, and between the two of them managed to get it wrapped in the towel. At the time, neither of them truly registered that the action figure was moving on its own. Ethan ran for twine, while Nathaniel wrestled with the bundle. After it was tied up, they put it in a trash bag, wrapped the excess trash bag around the bundle, and tied the bag with twine. That new bundle went into another trash bag and out to the metal trash barrel. The lid was quickly latched and then double-checked. Nathaniel and Ethan agreed to keep silent about the incident. They had work to do.

****

The evening had worked out perfectly tonight. Ethan had gotten all the tents set up in record time, helped by guests who usually stood by and watched. Nathaniel had no problems with or complaints from guests. The youngest child in the group was ten-years-old, so Nathaniel had been able to get a little spookier in the story-telling. The food came out perfect. The guests were happily mingling with some starting to head back to the tents. No eerie goings-on or mythical creatures crashing the party.

He did not count the thumping that had been coming from the trash barrel all evening as eerie. After all, he knew what it was. The unnerving possessed piece of plastic had an active streak. He couldn't wait to get the toy imp to the landfill the next morning. He and Ethan exchanged a cautious glance as they went to the trash barrel with the evening's waste. Eerie? Nope. Alarming? Yes. Ethan took a deep breath and lifted the lid like a shield that he peeped from above.

The doll was standing in the middle of the barrel looking up with alternately flashing eyes. It still looked five inches tall. It had chewed through the towel, twine, and garbage bags. The thumping they had heard was the result of it jumping to try to move the lid. Now, the action figure bared its fangs and crouched as if to leap. Their reaction was to immediately dump the filled trash bags on top of it and slam the lid down and latch it on. Then they double-checked that the lid was latched properly. Nathaniel actually jumped to sit on top of the barrel as if to help hold the lid in place. Then he thought of action figure fangs directly below his bottom and jumped off.

"Those were some nasty choppers," said Ethan.

****

After the guests had left the following morning, Nathaniel and Ethan stood next to the trash barrel beholding it for a long time. They could see the new dent in the middle of the lid that had not been there the evening before. As they watched, the next thump from the action figure occurred. It sounded louder than before. They knew they had to take the trash to the landfill. That could not happen until the lid came off. As the barrel was chained to the ground, taking the whole thing was not an option. Another hit to the lid.

Ethan went back to the building and found an old canvas sack. He held it over the barrel while Nathaniel cautiously unlatched and lifted the lid. They both had shaking hands. The fanged figure ended up jumping directly into the sack. Ethan quickly tied the top of the sack into a knot. The action figure was now about 10 inches in height from the size of the struggling item in the sack. It had simply climbed up the other trash bags to reach the lid easier. A tear was starting to appear in the sack along the seam from the scuffle the action figure was putting up. It honestly sounded like it was chewing.

A ripping sound came from the sack and the doll exploded out of it. It landed in the dirt and skid to a stop a few feet away. This was the moment it decided to act like an action figure. It slowly pushed itself up and turned around, focusing its flashing blue eyes on Nathaniel. It bared its fangs. It crouched. It snarled as it pounced directly at Nathaniel's face. Nathaniel instinctively swung the barrel lid that he still held. The lid connected and sent the action figure flying across the area by the trash barrel. The doll flew right through the open door of the building. The men gave each other a panicked look and ran to the door, dropping both the lid and the sack in their hurried alarm.

****

Nathaniel and Ethan grasped that they faced one of their worst childhood nightmares. Something playful that had allowed their imaginations to expand now had a mission of its own. Except this particular toy did not belong to either of them. Nor had either of them imagined as children, ever, action figures that could chew through towels and attack real humans with plastic knives. Nor had any of their toys grown in size in a short period of time. Cassandra had once shrunk a teddy bear in the wash, but grown? Nope. Never.

The two stood outside on opposite sides of the doorframe and meekly peeked into the building. The layout included several areas with plenty of places someone their size could hide. It would be even easier for a ten-inch being. They could not even see the corners from their lookout. Glancing up, they appeared to wonder at the same time if it could be slinking above them. They did not see anything. Nathaniel remembered once telling his mother that he was not afraid of the dark. He was scared of anything that might be in the dark. At mid-morning, the building was not dark, but it wasn't light either. Where would that thing hide? Maybe they could ignore the closed off bathroom and bedroom. Could the doll open doorknobs? From somewhere in the dim recesses came a discordant pitter-pattering.

"I hope that is a giant rodent," Ethan mumbled. "Or a baby Bigfoot." Nathaniel chuckled nervously.

With a wary look toward each other, they stepped inside the building and closed the door. After it clicked shut, Ethan realized they had not looked behind it first. He whirled around, and almost slumped with relief when he saw nothing there. He looked above him again and into the corners to his right and left. Nothing was there. Then he glanced at his partner. Nathaniel was standing stock still and staring into the open area of the room. Ethan followed his gaze.

The doll's eyes were flashing in their direction from the middle of the table. It stood holding a kitchen knife in one hand. The other hand was at its side, opening and closing regularly. It was now about fifteen inches in height. It looked very menacing for its size. They stared at each other for several moments. Nathaniel had time to see it was the knife they used to chop the onions before the doll moved.

The action figure tilted the knife and held it like a spear. It started running to the edge of the table. It leapt from the end of the table, the point of the knife flying directly at Ethan's chest. Ethan jumped to the side and shoved himself and Nathaniel to the floor. They scrambled up to find the knife stuck in the wood of the door and the action figure hanging by one hand from it. Ethan and Nathaniel were near the cleaning supplies and desk. Ethan grabbed a broom and Nathaniel a box of rubber bands. The men looked at each other, nodded, and turned to notice that the doll was no longer hanging from the knife. The knife was no longer stuck in the door, either.

The doll was kneeling in the middle of the table with the bent knife dropped at its feet, and both hands in fists. It was baring its fangs while emitting a low growl. It took a running start and jumped to land at the end of the broom. Then it began to crawl up the broomstick while Ethan furiously tried to shake it off. *THWACK!* Nathaniel hit the doll in the head with a large rubber band. The doll lost its balance but quickly regained it. *THWACK! THWACK! THWACK!* The next three rubber bands slowed it down enough for Ethan to run to the table and start banging the broomstick against it. The doll lost its grip on the broomstick. It rolled away and stood up, hands against its legs, panting. It seemed a bit smaller from all the movement. The flashing eyes and fangs were no less intimidating. It was soon ready to go again.

The doll straightened up in the middle of the table. *THWACK!* This time it did not even flinch. Instead, the action figure looked right toward Nathaniel, crouched and jumped. It landed on Nathaniel's hand, sending the fangs deep into his thumb. Nathaniel yelled and dropped the rubber bands. Then he used his other hand to squeeze the action figure's head until it let go. He flung the action figure onto the middle of the table, where it skidded to a stop and did not move for several seconds.

The doll stood itself up in the middle of the table. The focus of it flashing eyes was on Ethan. Ethan got a better grip on the broom. Out of the corner of his eye he saw Nathaniel grab a metal yardstick. The action figure was noticeably smaller now, and the two felt they might have a chance to get rid of the toy. The doll bent down and picked up the forgotten knife. It gave Ethan a disturbing smirk full of sharp teeth.

Then Cassandra brought down the 10-inch cast iron skillet on the sinister plaything's head. The action figure stumbled around a bit before dropping. The doll was now perfectly still at the edge of the table, exactly like a doll is supposed to be. When the action figure started to stir again, Cassandra used the skillet again and again and again until the doll was in pieces scattered across the table. Then she hit it with the skillet one more time for good measure. And one last time just because it felt good. She then very carefully set the skillet down next to the pieces. Nathaniel and Ethan stared at her wide-eyed and with jaws dropped open. Both still held their makeshift weapons ready to swing.

That morning, she had decided it would be nice to take some freshly baked cinnamon rolls to the men for breakfast. Things had been going pretty well at the campsite lately, and they deserved a treat. More honestly, she wanted a cinnamon roll, but didn't want to eat alone. She had heard the fracas all the way out to the car. She had run to the building, opened the door, and seen the struggle with the unnatural little figurine. Looking around, she had grabbed the first thing she could use as a weapon and helped out. No one messed with her son or his friend.

"I brought cinnamon rolls," she told the astounded two, and went to retrieve them.

****

Cassandra had developed a healthy respect for sharks after watching *Jaws* as a child. Not just respect, but admiration. Seriously, sharks were swimming around before trees came into existence. Gratefully, she knew sharks were not a problem in the middle of the North American continent. Then again, what was a rogue great white shark compared to an action figure with fangs?

Mist

Hydration is incredibly important in minimizing altitude sickness. Altitude sickness usually starts between 5,000- and 8,000-feet altitude. Simply going to a lower altitude and trying not to exercise too much will help. Symptoms can include sleepiness, dizziness, upset stomach, headaches, and shortness of breath.

These, of course, are the same symptoms experienced when exposed to fae mists.

Nathaniel's Firepit was located at 6,795 feet in altitude. He and Ethan always handed out water bottles to every person as soon as they arrived. They had a way to get people help if any of the guests started feeling sick or was injured.

Except, fae mists cause ailments not curable with human medicine. Thankfully, anyone who comes into contact with them eventually recovers. Unless a person chooses to go through the mists. Then the person will be lost.

****

Every once in a while, children that were considered funny and spirited by their parents showed up at the camp. The truth? The sarcasm was not funny. Their actions could put other guests in danger. They were disruptive. Nathaniel would then ask guests to get their children to show appropriate behavior, or leave. This time, though, the brat fell sick. He had been wandering near the edge of the woods. Ethan had gone to retrieve him and seen him walking through a ground mist. In a couple of hours, the guests had been sent to an urgent care center for the kid. With a case of altitude sickness, it was unlikely those particular guests would ever return.

The next morning, after the other guests had left, Ethan went back to check out the area he had found the brat wandering in. He and Nathaniel were going to leave in a few minutes. Something had seemed odd about the mist. When Ethan got to the area, he saw that the mist had spread. This was unusual, especially when it had been a bit dry and the temperatures were up. Ground mist did not really occur in this area, though there could be occasional fog. Ethan touched it. It felt clammy and had the consistency of confetti. This was probably another paranormal thing. He'd better warn Nathaniel.

****

Nathaniel felt, rather than heard, movement behind him. He turned, saw who it was, and smiled. "Hey, mom." Then he frowned. Something was not quite right. The woman standing there looked a lot like his mother, but it definitely was not Cassandra.

"You can see me?" she asked. Her voice had kind of bell-ringy undertone to it.

"Yes. You look just like my mother," Nathaniel confirmed.

"Is your mother named Cassandra?" Nathaniel nodded and the woman continued, "She is my daughter. That makes you my grandson. I am named Miabria. What are you named?"

Her manner of speaking was strange, but he answered, "Nathaniel." Grandmother? Cassandra had always told him that she was not sure what had happened to his grandmother. Now she was standing here. He supposed he would need to take her to Cassandra. He did not want to as Miabria was giving him the creeps.

"Who are you talking to?" asked Ethan from the doorway. Nathaniel just shook his head. Ethan shrugged, then decided he needed to go home anyway. He was feeling sleepy, and his stomach hurt. Talking about the mist could wait. Nathaniel watched Ethan drive off and turned back to his grandmother. Miabria was watching Ethan with a speculative look.

She turned back to Nathaniel, "I bet that boy is a hard worker."

Nathaniel chose not to respond, instead saying, "That's my car. I will take you to Cassandra."

****

Cassandra saw Nathaniel drive up. When she noticed his passenger, she almost screamed. Her father had warned her this might happen. But it had been more than fifty years since he had rescued her. She had sincerely thought her mother would never show up. She did not have time to call for Belinay before Nathaniel and Miabria were coming in the front door.

Miabria looked around in disgust. The house did not meet her standards. Then she turned to Cassandra, "Where is Dumitru?"

Cassandra smirked and said, "Nowhere that you can get to him now." Nathaniel was confused. Why not tell Miabria that his grandfather had gone to the in-between a couple of years back? But he wisely said nothing.

"I came through an area where I found your son. I could sense your presence there. You will return with me to be with your family. I can tell that your son is only half human, so he should come as well, though he will have to work for favor."

"No," said Cassandra. "Leave. Now. You are not welcome. You do not have an invitation to come to my house or that of my son. You may not enter either of our vehicles or go into any building or structure where either of us is at." Miabria's eyes flared with lightning, but she turned, left the house, and started walking up the road.

Cassandra looked at Nathaniel and explained, "My mother is Fae. I know I have told you this before, but you refused to believe me. The Fae cannot do anything they have been told not to do by another Fae. Also, they can usually only be seen by those with Fae ancestry and ghosts. If they choose to be seen by others, it is because they want to cause harm. Miabria tricked my father into going to the fae lands from Romania. When I was born, he found a way to return and brought me with him. He did not want me to grow up in the fae lands. He entered in 1870 and came out in 1973. He brought us both to the United States, thinking we would be safe here. It took a lot of work and learning for him, but Belinay and Cheshire helped."

How could he be gone more than a hundred years?" asked Nathaniel.

"The fae lands are not another planet like what is in the portal at the campsite. They are a parallel universe, and time does not pass at the same speed," Cassandra explained.

Nathaniel shook his head. It was too much to absorb. Then he looked at his mother and said, "I will drive us to the jailhouse to talk to Cheshire. We can call up Belinay there. And we should all go to check up on Ethan."

****

As it turned out, Belinay was already with Cheshire. She had visited the campsite the night before to hear Nathaniel's story. The story had been about ghosts. Overnight, she had played tricks on teenagers who had looked bored. She had not noticed the mist until the next morning when Ethan had waded into it. She had debated between going to Cassandra and Cheshire. In the end, she chose Cheshire so they could debate how to tell Cassandra.

"Miabria came to my house. It took decades for her to find me. Though it was probably only a couple of days on her end. She knew exactly where I am," Cassandra just jumped in with the information. As she looked between Belinay and Cheshire, she realized they already knew.

They both stumbled over each other's words in apologizing. Then they tried to explain how they wanted to help her but didn't know how. Then they went into a catalogue of the many times either of them had dealt with the mist.

"Cool," Nathaniel finally interrupted. "This is incredibly fascinating. But I am worried about Ethan. I think he was touching the mists." They all looked at him. Ethan had been alone since his girlfriend broke up with him. If the mists had made him sick, he would be suffering by himself.

"I am coming with you," piped up Detective Nickel. Once again, they had all forgotten about him. "I have nothing better to do anyway."

****

Ethan's apartment was tiny, and with all of them there, it was crowded. Ethan became worried right away. There was no reason for all of them, including the Detective, to be here if a serious problem was not happening. He would bet it had something to do with the mist at the campsite.

"You look really, really awful," said Belinay.

"You look dead," answered Ethan. " I don't know what hit me." Even answering wore him out. He just wanted to go back to sleep. Whatever was happening out there, he did not care right now. Someone else could deal with it this time.

"You must have touched the fae mist. My mother, Miabria came from the fae lands looking for me. Whenever the two parallel worlds open, a slightly toxic mist forms that can make people sick. Even if it doesn't touch your skin, or you don't inhale it, you will feel sick," Cassandra explained it to him, thinking that he did look really, really awful. "We need to get back to the campsite to try to get Miabria to go back to the fae lands. We cannot actually force her to go, but I want to try. I don't think we can trick her. The Fae are exceptionally intelligent."

Detective Nickle looked like he was sorry for his choice to come along.

Cheshire and Belinay nodded. They did not tell the others it was possible that Miabria could bring other Fae through in order to get her way. She was not powerful in the fae lands, but likely still had friends. Like all Fae, when she wanted something, she would do whatever it took to get it. She wanted her daughter back.

By silent agreement, they all started for the door. The campsite awaited. Ethan stood, then sat back down again. He bent down and held his head in his hands.

"I do not think I can make it," stated Ethan since he could barely breathe. "I do think I will be fine on my own. Really." The others traded looks. They decided the same thing. Miabria needed to be banned from the entire area, and Ethan would not be helpful in his condition. He was a big boy. He could deal with being a bit sick.

They all still felt guilty about leaving him anyway. At least he could avoid being seen in Cheshire's van.

****

"What happens if the mist touches buildings?" asked Nathaniel when he saw the ground completely covered with mist around the building and the campsite. The only spot open was a circle around the firepit.

"Nothing," Cheshire said. "It is just a harmless chemical to inanimate objects. But anything alive can get sick, including plants and myself, unless you have Fae ancestry. See the trees look a bit blue-tinged. Detective, you really should stay in the van. It won't impact you, Nathaniel, because you are part Fae." Detective Nickel took a long look at the ground and stepped out of the van to join the others.

Belinay floated above the ground mist, but the rest tip-toed gingerly through it. They concentrated so much on the ground that Cassandra almost ran into Miabria. They stared at each other, neither wanting to be the first to speak. Miabria was first, "You need to return home. That is your place. Stop this nonsense and let us go back. Your son comes too."

"This is my home. I have not known anywhere else my whole life. My son stays," answered Cassandra, the lightning from her anger showing in her eyes. "We refuse to go with you."

"You are not to come anywhere to this world ever again!" Nathaniel was livid. Miabria turned to him in shock. He had just confined her to the fae lands for as long as the two worlds existed.

Because they were all standing in the mist, Miabria was visible to all. The mist would not allow Miabria to hide. Cheshire and Detective Nickel both took a step back when she turned to them. Her voice took on a strange tone, "Would either of you be interested in coming with me? My home is stunning. Everything is plentiful. The weather is always perfect. Luxuries abound. You can be valuable to our society. You would be treasured by me. This will be the last time I can offer anyone this. Come with me."

Nathaniel had childhood memories of Dumitru telling him about those not born in the fae lands. These outsiders were not treated well. Often outsiders did all the work that none of the fae-born wanted to do. Outsiders would get lured to what appeared as a beautiful land. It would turn out to not be any better than this side. In many cases, it was worse. Basically, the Fae were lazy and took it out on outsiders, often in a very mean manner. They loved to tell lies about how wonderful everything was. He had no intention of crossing the mists.

Detective Nickel started forward. Miabria locked eyes with him.

"Don't do it," said Cassandra. "The mist you have been walking through can make it easy to hypnotize you. The lightning in her eyes causes you to focus on her and not reality. Things will look better than they are. Can you hear me? Please say you can hear me."

But Detective Nickel wanted the fae tale.

Miabria stepped back and held out her hand to Detective Nickel. As she did so, the mists parted from around her. He had a clear view of the parallel world she came from.

He saw stunning parks with a perfect driveway leading to the castle of his dreams. The brightness of the colors mesmerized with their beauty. He took a step towards them and then took a second one. Suddenly he felt Cheshire's arm around his waist holding him from going forward. This caused him to look away, and get a side view. For a second, he saw the fields, looking no more attractive than on this side of the mists. The far-off castle needed repair. The driveway to it was dirt. The colors seemed less bright. When he looked at it straight-on, it was lovely again, which seemed wrong somehow. In that moment of hesitation and confusion, Cheshire pulled him back. He watched in desperation as the mists closed again, then dissipated. He would not be going.

And Miabria would not be coming back.

****

Ethan decided he would stay away from unusual mists from now on. Only the natural ones for him. Or not. No mists were fine with him. He could feel the heavy air that came right before a storm. That would be pleasant. It could wipe away the rest of the haziness.

Summer was coming to an end, and Cassandra could smell the storm in the air. She trusted it would not bring hail. Or maybe, just enough hail to kill the weeds in the yard? A bit of thunder and lightning could be exciting. She would love to curl up on the couch with a cup of honeyed coffee and listen to a late evening summer storm.

Detective Nickel did not come into work for a couple of days. The mist had only made him slightly sick, but decided that it wasn't worth it to go. He admitted that the word "work" was an exaggeration. No one missed him. His worldview had shifted with the mists. He wondered if he would always regret not going to the fae world. He was alone here. He had no close family and never really became friends with anyone. He could not say he actually had a career. He trusted Cheshire, though, and knew there was a reason that he'd been held back. Maybe, it was time he connected with others a bit more.

Nathaniel still did not like Detective Nickel, but would not have wished the consequences of going to the fae world on him. He was still adjusting to meeting his fae grandmother, although he was glad she had returned to her homeland. He and Cassandra had a long conversation. He now understood why she had stayed in this dimension as a human. He was also grateful, sort of, that he had some of the powers of his mother's people. Maybe one day he would understand his father's.

Belinay floated around the jailhouse office chatting with Cheshire. Cheshire had spent several hours incredibly dizzy, but had recovered from his contact with the mist. Both felt the coming storm and realized what it meant. They were not concerned. The coming storm was a good thing and both had dealt with it in previous cycles.

Outside, a drizzle started.

The Storm

"Gully washer" was one of the first phrases that Dumitru learned when he and Cassandra made it to the United States. The term was not unique to one area, and he had loved the imagery it portrayed. It was also a perfect description of the late summer storms that could appear in the area they had finally settled in. The rain in these storms comes down so hard it seems like a person is looking through a sheer curtain. The streets run with water a couple of inches deep. The thunder varies from long rumblings to sharp cracks that make a person jump. The lightning sometimes comes so often the room one is in stays almost constantly lit. Afterward, the air feels cleaner, with the smell of wet soil saturating the atmosphere.

When Nathaniel was about three-years-old, his grandfather taught him the term. For about a year after that, every time there was even the slightest sprinkling, Nathaniel would run around yelling, "I think it's a gully washer!"

The storm that came to the area that day, however, was not in any way, shape, or form a natural event. Those that experienced it would always refer to it in the future as "The Storm from Nathaniel's Firepit's Opening Year."

****

Cheshire and Belinay showed up at Cassandra's house late that evening. She was expecting them. "This is the finalizing storm, isn't it?" She could tell the coming storm was different. This was not her first cycle. However, she was not as sensitized to the elements as Cheshire. Cheshire simply nodded.

"I went to tell Nathaniel and Ethan to meet us at the campsite," Belinay said. Cassandra smiled thinking that with a friendly ghost, one did not need a phone. Nor could Belinay be ignored or sent to voice mail. Belinay could not be ignored, period.

Cassandra insisted on driving. She was so ready for this.

****

Nathaniel and Ethan were chatting by their vehicles. The drizzle was not heavy enough to get them wet. They both looked towards Cassandra's car when she came up the drive. Both of them were full of curiosity. Belinay had not told them why they needed to be here right away. As usual, they simply did as she told them. They had each driven as quickly as possible, and arrived at the campsite full of concern. The first thing they did was to search the site for something unusual. Relieved to find nothing, they had headed back to the vehicles to wait.

Cassandra jumped out of her car, her excitement shining through in the inability to stand still. Her whole being was vibrating with eagerness. Belinay went to the two men and grinned at them, also seeming unusually animated. Cheshire went straight to the firepit and began working to start the fire. Cassandra and Belinay soon followed the path to the firepit. Then Belinay turned back, looked at Nathaniel and Ethan, and said, "Well, come on!" The men looked at each other, shrugged, and followed. They both figured someone would eventually tell them what was going on. If not, they had learned that anything out there would make itself known.

****

As soon as the kindling took hold, the drizzle turned into rain. As the fire grew, the rain came down harder. The fire continued crackling without the rain impacting it. Nathaniel, uncomfortably soaked through, finally said, "Is anyone planning to tell me why we are here?"

Silence.

"Did you hear me?" asked Nathaniel.

More silence. He threw his hands up and longingly looked at the building. Ethan was not a happy camper either.

When the firepit was going hot, Cheshire turned to the two men, "All the events here lately are related to the portal. You know that already. The events are cyclical. At the end of the cycle, there is a storm that will end the events, for a while anyway. It is an incredible thing to experience. Not only does it mean a temporary stop to all these crazy phenomena, but it boosts every one of your senses."

Then, they all sat down on the benches surrounding the firepit to wait. Nathaniel and Ethan continued to glance at the building, both wishing they at least had a hat. Neither was willing to try to get a jacket, apprehensive of how Belinay might hold them back. Cassandra and Cheshire seemed unaware that the rain had drenched them all the way through.

The rain came down even harder. The fire burned even brighter. At that point, the lightening started.

****

The first lightning strike was pink and landed somewhere in the parking area. No thunder followed. The second and third were yellow and landed behind the building in the nearby woods. Still no thunder was heard. After that, numerous color strikes grew closer and closer to the firepit. Despite the danger that lightning poses to those outside without shelter, no one felt frightened. The abnormal light display did not feel electric. It was felt through their beings as a warmth spreading from their fingertips to their core down through the rest of their bodies and back out. The pulsating thermal sensation felt pleasant.

The lightening that struck the firepit was purple and green. It caused the fire in the pit to flare up twenty feet high. The remarkable sight, full of several colors – shining, twirling, sparkling, dancing – through the air, continued for quite a few minutes. Then, everything seemed to freeze in time. The group felt frozen as well, not breathing and unable to move.

WHOOSH! The flames collapsed on themselves. The fire simply went out and the lightning around them ceased.

Suddenly the group found themselves unconstrained by the storm. When the group moved closer to the firepit they noticed three things. First, the air was the exact temperature each most preferred. The idea of varying perfect temperature occurred to them even though none of them would have thought of it before. Second, the colors around them were vivid, and the sounds from the rain formed a fine tempo. Third, they all felt an overwhelming sense of contentment.

The firepit circle itself looked like your average dirt-floored, sooty, firepit circle. No portal showed at the bottom. No one would suspect that it had filled a summer with magical beings and weird goings-on.

Not knowing what else to do, most of the group headed back to the building for towels to dry off and hot drinks. Belinay stayed near the firepit, reminiscing about another storm and a man named Lockerton.

Epilogue

Cassandra, Belinay, Cheshire, Nathaniel, and Ethan sat around the firepit. Detective Nickel had joined them but seemed uncomfortable socializing. The five that could eat were chock full of grilled goodies along with brownies with vanilla bean ice cream and homemade strawberry topping. Belinay was glowing, relishing her time with her friends, though she sorely wished she could still eat.

The group enjoyed themselves in the early autumn evening. Nathaniel and Ethan had cleaned up the site and building, stored benches and equipment, and closed down the campsite for the winter. It would open again in the late spring.

The discussion had been about whether it would be a good idea to reopen. It was a side hustle for Nathaniel and Ethan, so the money was not a need for anyone. Then again, the campsite business was booked out for quite a while.

The storm had ended the cycle, but it was a cycle. That meant it would start up again. Someday. If it had been the firepit itself that had restarted the cycle, then they would have these situations every year. Or the storm could have shut it down for decades. No one knew what had started or ended the cycle in the past.

For that matter, no one was completely sure the cycle HAD ended.

Finally, Nathaniel spoke up. He had been thinking of the excitement that had been added to his rather routine life. "Yeah, I think I WILL keep the campsite going. It has already become one of the better mistakes I have made in my existence. What do you think, Ethan?" Ethan grinned and nodded.

Acknowledgements

Haggis Wildlife Foundation: I have no earthly idea what algorithm led me to your page from watching John Cusack. I am so happy that it did. I have spent hours watching your "mockumentaries," and they always make me smile. I do wish I had a tartan nest.

My family, who loves me anyway.

Amanda, who convinced me to start writing again. Just the kick in the pants that I needed to get past my dreary life.

Susan, Karla, Mike, Jeannie, Ashley, the book club, and any I have missed who have supported me. (Some without a clear knowledge of my writing skills.)

And the action figure chapter? That was inspired by Steven Spielberg. Obvious to those who know my taste in movies.

Author Bio

Rebecca A. Espinoza has been writing since she was a child. She first won in a writing contest in eighth grade. Since then, she has written for smaller publications and several opinion pieces. She was a Denver Post Voices Columnist in 2014. She continued writing for herself.

When she started to get bored with life, someone convinced her to start putting it into a book, or books. This is her first published book.

The author lives in Northern Colorado.